# Nobody Kills Uncle Buster and Gets Away With It

# Nobody Kills Uncle Buster and Gets Away With It

## Susan Koehler

turtle cove press
**Tallahassee, Florida**

Paperback ISBN: 978-1-947536-07-4
Ebook ISBN: 978-1-947536-08-1

Library of Congress Control Number: 2021935383


Printed in the United States of America
The text of this book was typeset in Palatino Linotype and ABeeZee.
Cover art and interior illustrations Copyright © 2021 by Shelby Koehler

10 9 8 7 6 5 4 3 2 1          1 2 3 4 5 6 7 8 9 10

**Also by Susan Koehler**

*Dahlia in Bloom*

*For my sisters, Joan, Judy, and Shirley,*
*who share this life with me*

# One

The phone rings in the kitchen and I'm thinking, *Who uses the landline anymore? It's gotta be a scam.* But Mom yells from the garage, "Sam, get the phone, please!" So I do.

"Hello?"

"Is this the Parsons residence? Home of Eva Parsons?"

"Yes."

"Oh, this must be Samuel. My, you sound so grown up. You must be nine or ten now."

"Um, twelve," I say. "And you must be..."

"Oh, forgive me. It's your Aunt Bess, sweetheart."

Aunt Bess. My mind opens a dusty file folder containing the aunts of West Virginia. Bess of Mercer County and older sister Bertie of Boone County. Not my aunts, actually. My mom's crazy aunts. My great-aunts. My not-so-great-aunts. Sweet tea, cheek pinching, moth balls, crochet doilies....

"Sam? Are you still there?"

"Oh, yes ma'am. I'm sorry."

"I need to speak to your mother. Or maybe you can pass along the message. It's about her Uncle Buster, dear. Uncle Buster is dead. You let her know, okay? Bye now."

"Wait, wait. Don't hang up! Please—"

*Click.*

And just like that, I'm the one who has to tell her.

1

# Two

Mom walks into the kitchen, loaded laundry basket tucked under one arm, hair tucked behind her ears. "Robo-call or wrong number?" she asks. She plops the laundry basket on the kitchen table and commences folding towels.

"Um, neither," I say.

She stops. Turns. Makes eye contact. "Was it important?"

I lead in gently. "It was Aunt Bess."

Immediately, the corners of her mouth tighten and her green eyes look glassy.

"Sam, is it about Uncle Buster?"

"Mom, she said he died."

Mom jukes to the right and then to the left, like she's looking for an escape. But there's no outrunning it. Finally, she gives up. Sinks into a kitchen chair and sobs into a clean washcloth.

Uncle Buster, mountain man of North Carolina. Can't say I ever got to know him all that well, even though we visited every summer. He didn't talk much. Caught fish in a creek behind his house. Liked blueberries so much he planted them right outside his front door. "He was cool, Mom. I'm really sorry."

"He was so special to me," she says between sobs.

*He was cool? You're an idiot, Sam.* Important mental folder here. He took her in after her parents were killed in a car crash. She was 16. She lived in that house with him. Finished high school and went to college nearby.

"I'm really sorry, Mom." I should do something. But what?

"I *knew* something was wrong," she says. She sits up straight, wipes away tears.

And I'm thinking, *Here we go.* For almost two weeks Mom's been trying to call Uncle Buster. He's not exactly one to sit by the phone. He likes to be outside, can't hear well, no cell phone, no internet. The man's hard to reach. But somehow Eva Parsons and her psychic-conspiracy-theorist tendencies deduced that something bad happened.

"I called both Aunt Bess and Aunt Bertie. Neither one is more than a few hours away. I begged them to drive down and check on him."

I pull out a chair and sit.

"Aunt Bertie said she called that odd Carl fellow who moved in across the road. She asked him to check on Uncle Buster, but who knows if you can trust him. I should have gone. I knew something had happened. I even dreamed about it." She dissolves into tears again.

The dream. He was in his favorite yellow chair. Suddenly he was drooling, foaming at the mouth, and gripping his stomach in pain. He was pleading for help. But she couldn't help him. Dad and I had listened to the play-by-play of this nightmare quite a few times already.

Mom takes a deep breath. "I'll call Aunt Bess. Then we'll start packing. We'll head to Ashe County first thing in the morning."

3

*We?* Wait! Totally not fair. No way am I going. She whips out her cell phone before I have a chance to throw a block. I jump in anyway. "But Mom, Joey Sabatini is coming over Thursday! And Oscar, too! You said--"

She flips up the stop-talking palm. "Sam, this is family. Your friends will have to take a raincheck." She turns away. "Aunt Bess, it's Eva..." and the sobbing begins again.

I gotta find a way out of this. I've worked on forging a friendship with Joey Sabatini ever since I found out his dad works for the Jacksonville Jaguars. Finally, it's our shared interest in the NFL draft that drew him in. We're just two days away from putting a little wager on our first-round picks and establishing a meaningful friendship. And by *meaningful* in that I get a step closer to the Jags. There's no way I can leave tomorrow.

More sobbing. "Aunt Bess, that's so kind of you, but there's no way I'd miss Uncle Buster's funeral. You know what he meant to me." Mom's pacing all over the house, cell phone on speaker in her left hand. Her right hand is a flurry of activity, alternately tidying the house and packing her suitcase. In and out of rooms she wanders. Aunt Bess, her voice shrill and hollow over the speaker, is trying to convince Mom to stay home.

"Sweetie, we don't want you to make that long drive. Buster would understand. Bertie and I have everything under control."

"I insist," Mom says firmly. "You shouldn't have to handle all the details. If we leave Jacksonville by dawn, Sam and I should make it before supper time tomorrow."

I think fast. Come up with something she'll buy into. As soon as she's off the phone, I begin my lie. "Mom, there's no way I can miss school right now. I have a huge pre-algebra test on Friday. It's 40% of my grade. And I need to do well. I'm on the fence. I have an 88.9 in that class right now." She pauses, wrinkles her forehead. This is good stuff. I need to pile on the details.

"This test is even tougher than the last one. It's going to be 45 problems in 50 minutes. We're having a big review session in class on Thursday. I really need to be there."

"Well, bring your books with you and I'll help you study. I'm sure Mrs. Alvarez will let you make the test up next week," she adds with satisfaction. And she's back in action.

I can't let this slip away. I've worked so hard to make this happen. Joey Sabatini puts me just one degree of separation from *my* team. I follow Mom to the kitchen. Maybe it's because she's wearing her running shoes, but I'm getting winded trying to keep up with her.

"It's not that easy," I say to her back. "Mrs. Alvarez taught us things that aren't in the textbook. And she talks so fast, I can't get it all down. Today my pencil ran out of lead. That dark red mechanical pencil. You can't see the lead so you never know when it's about to reach the end."

I'm on a roll now. I know this is working. "I've arranged to meet with Mrs. Alvarez tomorrow at lunch. She's going to help me catch up on the notes I missed."

Mom stops moving and stares at the digital clock on the microwave. It's 4:45. What's so mesmerizing about that? Then she says, "We'll talk to your father when he's home from practice. We'll figure something out."

My dad is a history teacher and head football coach at St. Johns River High School. Spring football practice started yesterday, so until mid-May, he won't get home before 6:45. That gives me a couple of hours to shore up my plan. I look at Mom and frown, nod, add a cherry on top. "I think I'll go review my notes for tomorrow's lunch meeting."

"Okay," she says, "you do that. I need to text my department head at the community college and get my classes covered." Mom nods absently and walks away.

*Score.*

I pull my pre-algebra textbook, calculator, and spiral notebook out of my backpack and head for my room. I plop them down on my desk loudly enough for Mom to hear and then quietly close the door. After opening both books to random pages, I pull out my cell phone and text my best friend Oscar.

My mom is trying to sabotage our Thursday plan.

As usual, I get an immediate response.

Y?

6

> She wants me to go out of town with her. But I'm on it. I told her I have a math test Friday.

UR a boss.

> Waiting for my dad to get home. We'll see.

LMK if I can help.

I briefly explain the situation, determined not to reciprocate Oscar's obsession with text abbreviations. Once he has the details, his response catches me off guard.

IDK. MayB U should go.

> What?! Can you talk? Call me.

My phone immediately buzzes with Oscar's call. "How can you even suggest I should go? I'd miss our draft party with Joey. This is crucial!"

"Yeah dude, but your uncle just died. Seems harsh."

I can't believe what I'm hearing. I sit back in silence.

Finally, Oscar speaks again. "Remind me why Joey Sabatini is so important to you anyway."

"Oscar, I thought we were of one mind here. Joey Sabatini's dad is some kind of accountant for the Jaguars. He sees every game up in the club seats with former players, celebrities, air conditioning, tables full of food. Brisket, yeast rolls, dessert trays, bottomless shrimp cocktails...you name it!"

"How does that affect us?"

I can't believe I have to explain this. "Because if we get in good with Joey, then we'll be part of his squad and he'll invite us to go to games with him. We'll be in club seats with former players, celebrities, AC, shrimp cocktail… Oscar, this is our chance!"

"Okay, okay…" Oscar's using his talk-me-down-off-the-ledge voice. "But let's think of a viable Plan B, just in case."

I have no interest in any plan other than A, but I say, "Okay, what's Plan B?"

"You send me your picks for round one, and if Joey still wants in, I'll invite him to my house Thursday. We'll watch the draft here while you watch it up in mountain land, but we'll be texting the whole time."

Even though he can't see the gesture, I roll my eyes. "Huge problem, Oscar. Uncle Buster's house doesn't have cable, and finding Wi-Fi or even cell reception up in the sticks is next to impossible. The place is a digital dead zone."

"Dude, it's the 21st Century. There's connectivity everywhere."

"Yeah, but I've already used up my data for this month. Until May 1, I'm operating exclusively on Wi-Fi." Our simultaneous groans are followed by a few seconds of silence.

Finally, Oscar comes back with his calm voice. "Okay, okay, how about this: You send me your picks and I'll take care of the rest."

"Oscar, Joey said we'd put a little wager on it."

"A bet?"

"Yeah, just $20."

Deep breath. "Okay, I'll spot you $20."

"Hey, thanks!"

"Don't get sentimental. I know where you live."

Suddenly, I hear the front door close and the sound of my dad's gear being dropped on the tile. I pull back the phone. Check the time. It's only 5:30. She must've called him.

"Oscar, I gotta go. My Dad's home early. Time to put Plan A into turbo charge."

"Later, dude. But I still think Plan A is harsh!"

Ignoring that last comment, I end the call, tuck my phone in my back pocket, and slump to the kitchen. Dad is at the sink washing up. He dries his hands with a paper towel and then mops the sweat from his face.

"Sam," he says, "your mother's upset and it's a 500-mile drive. I hate to see her do this alone, and I just can't leave right now. Explain to me why it is you can't go with her."

He stands in front of the kitchen window, light creeping around his edges like the silver lining on a massive storm cloud. I plant myself in his shadow and feign my hopeless expression. "It's my pre-algebra test on Friday." Digging back through the details, I lay it all out for him. The red mechanical pencil, 45 questions in 50 minutes, the 88.9, 40% of my grade, the lunch meeting. I remember it all.

"That's interesting," he says. "Your mother called and filled me in. So I called Mrs. Alvarez. Nice lady."

"You called her?" My mouth is suddenly dry.

"Yeah. She doesn't know anything about a test on Friday. Or a red mechanical pencil. Or a lunch meeting.... And you have a 95 in that class."

*Busted.*

"I smelled a lie, son. Too many details. Go pack your suitcase."

# Three

After eight hours, three bathroom stops, and two fast food meals, we reach our exit to the two-lane highway and winding mountain roads that will eventually lead to Uncle Buster's place. Mom's conversational climate has bounced back and forth between droughts and floods.

"He was a frugal one, my Uncle Buster. Liked to feel self-sufficient. He built that house himself, you know. Over the years, the county came through and offered connection to county water lines. But no, Uncle Buster kept his well water. They offered garbage pick-up. But no, Uncle Buster piled garbage in the back of his truck and hauled it down to the solid waste management facility himself. So stubborn, that one."

"Uncle Buster has a truck?"

"Well, he did, but you might not remember. He traded it in several years ago when he found out he could get better gas mileage with a little compact car." She smiles and shakes her head. "Come to think of it, I don't know how he hauled his garbage after that. I'm sure he figured something out. He was very resourceful."

She's staring straight at the road ahead, but her eyebrows twist like pretzels and I feel like I need to find something to add to this conversation. Finally, I say, "I guess you can do what you want when you live by yourself."

"He didn't mind being alone, but oh, it made my aunts worry. For being his younger sisters, they sure are a couple of mother hens." She pauses momentarily, and I know what's coming next. "They were there just three weeks ago. Did I mention that?"

"I think so," I say. *Only about six times already.*

"They insisted on doing lots of cleaning." She sort of chuckles and shakes her head. Just like last time she told this story. About twenty minutes ago. "Uncle Buster never was one to prize tidiness. He was kind of a pack rat. But he always seemed to know where to find things." She sighs. It's like instant replay every time she starts this story again.

While she launches into Uncle Buster's account of the big cleaning fiasco, I'm lulled into mindlessness by the monotonous hills rolling past us along the highway. The same thing, over and over, except for an occasional house or herd of cows. Or goats. Why goats?

My mind drifts to Joey Sabatini. I sent my draft picks to Oscar, but I can't believe I'm missing my chance to get on the inside with Joey. Unless we hit a serious growth spurt, the closest Oscar and I will ever get to the game of football is fetching water or keeping stats. But that's okay. Because my ultimate plan is to be a sports reporter. An anchor. A commentator. I'll rattle off stats and offer the play by play. Getting into Jags' club seats with some legends could be essential to my career path!

The silence becomes awkward so I offer the same comment I've used twice already, hoping it still fits. "Well, that was nice of them to clean."

12

"He was so put out," she continues. "He called me after they left. He said they cleared out all kinds of papers and now he can't find them. I don't know what papers he could possibly need." She shakes her head. "Probably old receipts and newspaper clippings. He saved everything." She tears up again.

We reach the outskirts of town and stop at the Piggly Wiggly to pick up some supper. Mom doesn't want to arrive empty-handed. Fried chicken, biscuits, potato salad, and two jugs of iced tea. Sweet for the aunts; unsweet for us.

It's not long until we round a steep curve and see a red brick chimney rising out of the hillside. The curve continues, but we make a sharp left at a crooked metal mailbox that says "Route 6, Box 322" in white, hand-painted script. We head up the rocky driveway, trimmed along one side with a whole patch of blueberry bushes, and swing a sharp right around the crabapple tree toward the garage of Uncle Buster's one-story brick house. The garage door is closed, and the little fuel-efficient Buster-mobile must be safely tucked inside.

A long pink Cadillac is parked in the driveway. As we pull in behind it, our headlights reveal the personalized license plate. *BYE-BESS.* I get it. You read it when you see her pull away. Only this isn't goodbye for us. It's just the beginning.

The front door opens and a yellow glow pours from the house into the twilight, illuminating tiny insects swarming above folding lawn chairs on the front porch. Aunt Bertie tumbles through the doorway and takes a few steps in our direction. She stops, out of breath from the mild exertion.

Aunt Bess emerges slowly and stands on the porch, bathed in the light of incandescent bulbs. Her unnaturally dark brown hair curls in toward the folds on her neck.

Mom leans in and whispers, "Let's just take the food for now. We can come back for our suitcases later."

Hugs are awkward when you're carrying a couple of jugs of tea. But that doesn't stop them. The aunts take turns wrapping us in their ample girth, and the *eau de mothball* scent momentarily stifles my breath. Tears begin to flow. I follow the three sobbing women into the house and close the door behind me.

They move hurriedly through the living room and lead us into the kitchen. Food and tea are dropped onto the counter and tears are pushed aside for the sake of information.

"Who found him?" Mom asks.

"Well, after that Carl fellow refused to break into the house, I had to call the sheriff to come check on him," Bess says.

"You remember the Waverly family," Bertie adds. "That Frank Waverly is the sheriff now. How about that? Always such a handsome one."

Mom's forehead wrinkles with confusion. Either she doesn't remember Frank Waverly, or like me, she's wondering why this is a relevant detail.

"You wanted someone to break in?" Mom asks.

"Yes," Bess continues. "Honey, we couldn't make it down. Bertie had to work, and my real estate business has been hoppin' so that I just needed a few days to myself at my cottage." She pauses, smiles, takes a detour. "You know, I have a vacation cottage at Smith Mountain Lake."

Mom stares blankly and sort of nods, her eyebrows pretzeling again.

"But I just couldn't bring myself to relax. I was worried sick the whole time."

Mom coaxes Aunt Bess back on track. "So when did the sheriff find him?"

"On Monday afternoon," Bess says. She breaks down in tears. "He was sprawled out on the living room floor."

Mom glances toward the living room.

"Oh, there's no mess left now," Bertie says. "We cleaned it all up with some bleach and water."

Mom looks horrified. "What kind of mess was there?"

Bess again. "Oh honey, all signs lead to a heart attack. He seems to have struggled a bit. I guess he was trying to get to the phone."

"Struggled?" Mom asks.

Bertie begins the play-by-play. "We got here Tuesday morning. The orange doily I crocheted for his last birthday was knocked down into his chair. His Meals on Wheels container was dumped on the floor and food was spilled all over the throw rug." She flaps her arms wide in a dramatic gesture to outline the area. "Green peas and Salisbury steak."

"Salisbury steak was his favorite," Bess sobs. "You know, I set up the Meals on Wheels for him because he was looking kind of puny."

15

"Yes, I know," Mom says. "That was so kind of you."

"His feet were twisted, right over left," Bertie continues, "and he had vomited on the rug."

"They say that happens with heart attacks," Bess adds.

Mom nods. Silent tears fall from her eyes. I feel like I should do something, but I don't know what. So I stand there, frozen.

"Oh, honey," Bess says, putting an arm around Mom's shoulder. "We didn't want to see you suffer this way. That's why we wanted to take care of everything."

They sandwich her in a group hug. More sobbing.

Mom comes up for air and asks, "Where is he now?"

"Sweetheart, he's over at the Ashe County Funeral Home. We made all the arrangements today. We picked out a beautiful casket. Pecan wood. He would have loved it."

I can't imagine he has much of a preference at this point. My stomach growls. I remember I'm hungry, but I don't want to be rude.

"We can take you over there tomorrow if you want," Bertie says. "You've had a long day. You need to get some rest. Are you and Sam staying at the Mountaineer Inn?"

Uh-oh. This is awkward. Mom assumed we'd stay at Uncle Buster's house. Like we always do. But of course, the aunts aren't usually around when we visit Uncle Buster.

"Oh, um..." Mom struggles for words. Her face drains of color. "Yes, I guess we'd better go get checked in."

"All right then," Bess adds. "You just call us when you're up and about. No need to be in a hurry tomorrow. The funeral's not 'til Saturday."

They usher us toward the door. As we swat our way through the swarm of tiny bugs, Bertie calls out, "And thank you for the food!"

There's silence in the car as we back away from *BYE-BESS* and make our way down the drive. Mom stops at the mailbox and looks left around the sharp curve to make sure the road is clear. Our headlights illuminate a tall gray figure standing in the grass on the opposite side of the road. My mouth drops open, but no sound comes out.

Mom's head sweeps right as she lifts her foot from the brake. She sees him and shudders. "Oh, that Carl Leibowitz," she mumbles. "Such an odd fellow."

She hits the accelerator a little harder than usual, the Jeep lurches forward, and we're on the asphalt and headed back to civilization. Well, sort of. Before we round the next curve, I look back and see moonlight reflect off Carl's glasses as he watches us drive away.

# Four

The Mountaineer Inn is a one-story, red brick motel. All twelve rooms face the parking lot, and there's a box air conditioner protruding from every window. We're issued a green plastic rectangle with an actual metal key hanging from it. But it's all okay. Because just beneath the neon "Vacancy" sign are the words "Free Wi-Fi."

We sit cross-legged on the two twin beds and eat our third fast food meal of the day. There's no TV in the room, so it's unbearably quiet. Mom looks exhausted. I'm actually starting to feel guilty that I tried to get out of this. I'm glad she's not alone.

"Mom, I'm really sorry about Uncle Buster," I say, and I mean it.

She fights back tears and begins to talk. "My father was the oldest. You were named after him, Sam." She glances my way. "Of course, you knew that."

"Yeah," I say. "I'm sorry I never got to meet him."

"Oh, he would've loved you. My dad loved every sport, just like you. But he especially loved football. He and Buster were a couple of gridiron greats when they were in high school. They were just a year apart, and they were the only boys, so they were close." The tears come.

"It must've been hard for Uncle Buster when your dad moved away."

Mom sighs and wipes away tears with the back of her hand. "Well, my father went off to college. He had big dreams. Uncle

Buster said he just wasn't cut out for that. But one day when he was in town, he saw a Help Wanted sign in the window of the Blue Ridge Building Supply, and the rest is history." She nods and speaks so softly I'm not sure if she's talking to me or to herself. "You know, he just retired a few years ago. He had worked at the Building Supply for forty-five years."

"I guess he was happy around here," I offer, "since he never left this place."

She smiles. That's good. "Yeah, he never really left home. He built his own house on the family farm and stayed close to look after my grandmother. I was just a child when she passed away. Over the years, her old farmhouse started to fall apart. Uncle Buster finally had it torn down."

"How come your aunts didn't stick around here?" It's something I've never really thought about until now.

"Well, Aunt Bertie got married and moved to West Virginia. Aunt Bess was smitten with one of the groomsmen from the wedding, so she decided to move there, too. The romance didn't work out for her, but she became so successful in real estate that she never came back."

"Was all that before you moved here?" I ask. She doesn't talk a whole lot about it, but I'm curious. I hope I haven't gone too far.

"I was 16 when it happened." Her eyes stare straight ahead now, fixed on some distant, invisible point. "I was in shock. I had lost my parents, and I was an only child, like you. I felt alone in the world. But Uncle Buster let me know I wasn't alone.

He took time off from the Building Supply to come stay with me. He was the executor of the will, so he made the funeral arrangements, sold the house, paid off the mortgage, took care of the insurance...and took care of me."

I feel like I need to say something. "Wow. Your parents really trusted him, and he came through."

"Yes," she sniffs. "He made sure I had everything I needed. He set up a college fund for me and put the rest into a savings account." She smiles softly and looks down at her hands. "Then he asked me if I'd mind coming to live with him in the mountains."

I try to imagine how it would feel to suddenly be alone like that. To have everything ripped away – your parents, your home, the life you wake up to every day, all the things you expect to be there forever. But I don't want to imagine that. It hurts too much. Finally, I say, "Mom, I'm so sorry you had to go through all that."

She sits quietly now. No more tears. Just stillness. "It was hard at the time. Sometimes it's still hard. But Uncle Buster made sure I knew I was loved."

I feel like I should lighten the mood. "Well, I bet Uncle Buster was glad you stayed close-by for college."

She laughs. *Good move, Sam.* "Yes! Good ol' Appalachian State University. So close I could come back here whenever I wanted. I think he liked that."

"Did Uncle Buster go to games and watch Dad play football?"

"No," she shakes her head. "Getting Uncle Buster to venture out and join any crowds was next to impossible. But he read the paper and kept up with the team."

"I guess it was hard for him when you got married and moved back to Florida." I regret the words as soon as they leave my mouth. She's suddenly serious and her face drains of color. I try to reroute. "But I know he liked for us to visit every summer."

"Yes, he liked that." Mom swallows hard and takes a deep breath. "Why don't you get the first shower, and I'll call Dad."

"Yeah, sure," I say, and I'm trying my best to dig out of the hole I just created. "Maybe we can go out for breakfast tomorrow. Kind of take it easy. Spend a little time, just the two of us. They said there's no rush."

She smiles. "I'd like that. Where should we eat?"

In all the summers we've spent in Ashe County, I've never paid much attention as we breeze through this tiny town. A bunch of one-story brick storefronts, from what I recall. "Let's look around in the morning and pick something."

"Sounds good." She smiles again, but tears collect in her eyes. I stand up, gather our trash, and give her a hug.

After a lukewarm shower, I'm standing there toweling off and I can hear Mom on the phone through the hollow bathroom door.

"I don't know, Bob, something just didn't seem right. They were in such a hurry to get rid of us. And the cleaning...."

Silence for a minute. I slide on my sweatpants and Jaguars jersey and exit the tiny bathroom.

"But get this – when we left, that odd Carl Leibowitz was standing by the side of the road. Just standing there in the dark. There's something...almost sinister about him."

I can't hear Dad's end of the conversation, but I'm sure he's thinking what I'm thinking. Mom's psychic-conspiracy-theorist senses are tingling.

"I know, I know. Yes, always peculiar." She laughs. *That's it, Dad. Bring her down.*

"I'm sure you're right. How's spring practice going?" She's being polite. She doesn't care about football. "Uh-huh... Hmm... Oh, my." A few seconds of silence and then, "Love you too, Bob." She lays her cell phone on the 1960s-era nightstand between our beds. "So, how was the shower?"

"Refreshing," I say. I plop down on my bed and grab my cell phone. I key in the Wi-Fi code and hold my breath. It works. *Sweet.* I run through all the ESPN draft predictions and compare notes.

Most of the experts have Heisman-winning quarterback Marshall Mills being plucked up by the Jets. That's too obvious. I'm thinking they'll go for Mendez, a center the size of a bulldozer. Their QB has an arm; he just needs protection. The Jags have no chance for Mills, so the way I see it, we'll keep our QB and pick a wide receiver who can actually catch the ball. Oscar thinks we'll go for the O-line. Not sure what Joey Sabatini thinks. Time to check in.

> Greetings from North
> Carolina.

As always, Oscar responds immediately. In the shortest form possible.

> Sup?

> How's Plan B shaping
> up?

> Gr8.

> Is Joey going to your
> house for round one?

> Plan B now stands for
> BETTER. I'm going to
> Joey's house.

Full punctuation and no text abbreviations. Oscar's bragging. I take a minute to swallow the raging ball of jealousy that just formed in my throat. *Shake it off, Sam.*

> Sounds good. You have
> my picks, right?

> Mendez 2 Jets? Mills 2
> Phins? WR Sumi 2 Jags?
> U sure?

> Yep.

> I say Mills 2 Jets.
> Mendez 2 Jags.

> No way. Our O-line is
> strong. What does Joey
> think?

His picks are a secret.
He'll let me know
Thursday when I'm at
his house.

*Again with the bragging.* I'm about to abandon texting and call Oscar when suddenly, headlights blast through our beige curtains and I feel like I'm in the spotlight. Literally. I get a little spooked and toss the phone on the bed. Maybe we have a neighbor moving in, I tell myself. But only a moment after they arrive, the lights shrink away.

I rush to the window and ease the curtain back ever so slowly. I blink my eyes hard. How can it be? A long pink Cadillac is rounding the corner that heads back up the mountain. And just before it recedes into the darkness, I catch a glimpse of the license plate. *BYE-BESS.*

# Five

It's daylight and I've given up on trying to convince Mom that Aunt Bess was here last night. Actually, I'm starting to doubt it myself. If the queen of conspiracies doesn't buy it, maybe it's too far-fetched to be true.

I'm logged into the Wi-Fi and scanning NFL draft predictions. The first round begins tonight at 8 p.m. Somehow, I need to make sure we're back in this room no later than 7:59. According to Plan B, that's when Oscar will text from Joey's house. I'll be streaming draft coverage on my phone while we maintain digital communication throughout. It's like I'll be there at Joey's house with them. Kind of.

"I think I'm finally ready." Mom zips her suitcase after neatly folding her pajamas and packing them away. She looks over at my pile of clothes on the floor and I'm ready for a lecture. But she doesn't say anything.

I open the door and sweep my hand with a dramatic flourish. "Let's explore the culinary offerings of this town," I say.

Mom smiles. Good to see. I close the door and she locks it. "Can't lose this giant key chain." She chuckles, sliding the green plastic rectangle into her purse.

As we climb into the Jeep, Mom grabs a flyer off the windshield. "Even in the mountains," she sighs, and tosses the paper on the console. She has a thing about unsolicited advertising. The flyer, in all caps, practically screams up at me:

25

MOUNTAIN-AIRE HOMES
STOP BY OUR DESK AT WESTON REALTY.
SEE THE RENDERINGS.
YOU DON'T HAVE TO BE A MILLIONAIRE
TO ENJOY THE MOUNTAIN-AIRE!
RESERVE YOUR AFFORDABLE MOUNTAIN-AIRE HOME
TODAY!

There's a cheesy drawing of a bunch of nearly identical, fake-looking log homes standing in a flat, green field. In the background, the sun sets behind some awkward, paint-by-number mountains.

We drive past a little office called Weston Realty, and above it looms a billboard with a giant Mountain-Aire ad. Same message in all caps. Same cheesy picture. These guys need a better marketing team.

"I see a diner up ahead. Sign says it's open." Mom waits for a response.

Above the little brick building I see a flashing sign: FOUR SQUARE DINER. WE ARE OPEN. FREE WI-FI. "Looks great to me," I say.

Fifteen minutes after we order breakfast, Mom's carrying on a hushed but nonessential conversation with Dad, and I am giving up on finding the correct Wi-Fi password.

Our waitress is about ten years older than Mom, stick-thin, and wears a hairnet over the bleach-blonde spiral on the back of her head. Her name is Fanny. Really. I can't make this stuff up. First she thinks the password is the diner's phone number. Or maybe it's the phone number backwards.

She yells to the short-order cook. He's pretty sure it's the name of one of the owner's dogs, but the only one he can remember is Lefty. And the password is not Lefty.

I look up from my phone to see a scrawny, sour-faced lady gawking at us from a booth by the side wall. Streaks of gray stream through her long black hair. Dark circles hang like shadows under her sunken eyes. She's tapping her fingers on the table, and I'm trying not to stare at the dirt under her nails. I can just hear the judgment going on in her head. *City slickers. So absorbed in your phones you can't even look at each other.*

Shadow lady continues to stare, even when I'm looking right back at her. Unbelievably bold. Mom ends her phone conversation, and I'm glad to have someone to talk to. I lean forward and whisper, "Don't look now, but there's this creepy lady in the corner staring at us."

Mom immediately turns around. *Geez.*

"Oh, Sam, she's all alone. She's probably jealous that I'm having breakfast with a handsome young man." I try not to roll my eyes, but I can't help it.

Our breakfast plates arrive just in time. I dive into my pancake special, and Mom stirs fresh blueberries and cream into a bowl of steaming oatmeal.

Suddenly, she says, "Sam, I have an idea. Instead of going up to the house and coming all the way back to town with my aunts, how about we go to the funeral home ourselves. I want to see if there's anything I can take care of."

Fine by me. As we finish eating, the shadow lady gets up to leave. "I'll see ya later, Fanny," she mumbles.

"See ya, June!" Fanny calls from behind the counter. Mom pays our tab and we head into the parking lot, just in time to see June-the-shadow-lady driving away. Her small gray pick-up wears a magnetic sign on the driver's door: "Meals on Wheels."

"See, Sam," Mom says. "I bet she's a very nice person."

We drive about a mile to the funeral home and find a space in the predictably puny parking lot. Inside, Mom introduces herself to a guy with a name tag that says: BARNEY BALDWIN, FUNERAL DIRECTOR.

Barney looks a lot like Ernie, of Bert and Ernie fame, except that he's wearing a suit that could be a hand-me-down from a somewhat larger brother. Mom gets choked up telling him about how Uncle Buster took her in when her parents died, and how he was such a kind and funny man, and how she just can't believe he's gone.

Barney's face contorts into a super-sympathetic expression, and he gently reaches out for Mom's elbow with one hand while giving her a tissue with the other. This guy has skills.

We follow Barney into a room with a pecan-wood casket. The top half of the casket is open and there lies Uncle Buster. His face doesn't look real. It's caked with layers of make-up and looks more like a well-traveled clay road than my Mom's stubborn but friendly uncle.

He's wearing a white Oxford shirt with his usual blue jeans. You can barely see the jeans because his legs are hidden under the closed half of the casket. Uncle Buster's arms are tucked down tightly by his sides. It's awkward.

Mom looks shaken. I'm thinking she might be horrified by the make-up job, but she says, "This all just seems so fast. Was the autopsy already performed?"

Barney looks uncomfortable. "There was no autopsy. By state law, there's only an autopsy required if something about a death looks suspicious. Sheriff Waverly was here with the sister of the deceased. He confirmed it appeared to be a heart attack."

"That just seems so odd. I thought there was always an autopsy." Mom looks pale.

"Well, laws vary by state. In North Carolina, the State collects a vial of blood to examine. And if the executrix had requested it, we would have made certain an autopsy was performed," Barney says.

"Executrix?" Mom looks super confused.

"Yes," Barney says. "An executrix is a female executor of a will–"

"I understand the word," Mom interrupts, maybe a little too impatiently. "I just don't understand who, or how..." She's obviously been thrown off balance. Words are failing her.

Barney maintains his composure really well. In his eerily gentle voice he says, "She arrived Tuesday morning with the deceased's will in hand. The will names the executrix as Miss Elizabeth Munroe."

*AKA, Aunt Bess.*

# Six

We go straight back up to Uncle Buster's place and pull in behind *BYE-BESS*. The garage door is open, so we decide to slip past Uncle Buster's car and enter that way. As soon as we round the corner and step onto the concrete floor, we're met with a surprising sight: the back of a husky, dark-haired guy with his arms around Aunt Bess.

Mom stops in her tracks and clears her throat. The huggers repel from one another like the North ends of two magnets. Aunt Bess starts raining tears and says, "Thank you for consoling me, Jud. I know you loved Buster, too." Straight out of a soap opera.

"Sorry to interrupt," Mom says, still frozen in her spot.

Aunt Bess goes into action. "Where are my manners?" She escorts the husky guy toward Mom and says, "Eva, you remember Jud Waverly, don't you?"

"Yes, of course." Mom reaches out to shake his hand, some of the color returning to her face. I'm wondering just how many Waverly boys there are when I notice Mom giving me the eye.

I step forward and shake the guy's hand. "Hi, I'm Sam."

The three adults swap stories about Uncle Buster as they ease toward the door that leads into the kitchen. I look at my phone as a distraction. No bars. No surprise. Battery at 24%. All this searching for Wi-Fi must be a power-drain. I duck out to the Jeep to find a charger.

31

As I'm reaching across the driver's seat, I hear two things. One is the high-pitched twitter of some songbirds. The other is the low, rumbling sound of voices. The voices aren't close enough for me to make out the words, and the songbirds aren't helping my attempt at eavesdropping. I quietly pull myself out of the Jeep and stand on the running board to get a better look.

Across the road, I can just make out the form of Carl Leibowitz. He's almost nose-to-nose with a guy in a short-sleeve white dress shirt, skinny black tie, and blue jeans. Carl has a threatening scowl on his face, and the guy is backing away, holding his hands up in the air. I'm wondering if I should call the cops, but then I remember. No bars.

The skinny-tie guy backs up until he reaches a shiny white pick-up parked on the side of the road. He gets in, makes a U-turn right on that sharp curve, and heads back down toward town. Carl stands there in a cloud of dust, chest puffed out, arms crossed, watching until the guy's truck disappears. All I can think is, *This Carl dude could be dangerous.*

I shut the Jeep door and turn toward the house when I'm suddenly yanked backwards. I closed the charger cord into the door. *Nice, Sam.* I turn back around to free the cord and notice something I hadn't seen before. Loose dirt is sprinkled all over the ground next to the pink Cadillac. I'm curious. I walk past the car and stare at Uncle Buster's blueberry patch. I'm not a guy who regularly notices plants, but I swear there used to be a lot more blueberry bushes. It looks like every other one has disappeared, replaced with piles of loose dirt over barely disguised holes.

I hurry back through the garage and run smack dab into Jud Waverly on his way out. He's got a small key in his hand and a big frown on his face.

"Excuse me," I say.

He grunts in return. I get the feeling we're not going to be friends.

I watch through the garage window as Jud makes his way to the shed out by the creek, and then I head into the house. The familiar scent of blueberries and old books catapults my memory through years of summer vacations. But this isn't a vacation. Mom stands at the kitchen counter talking to the aunts. Bertie sits at the table eating cold chicken and drinking sweet tea. Bess hovers between Mom and the Blue Ridge Building Supply calendar that's hanging on the wall. I want to bring up the loose dirt and missing bushes, but this conversation looks serious.

"I know he never wore a tie, but when he went somewhere special he always put on a sport coat. At my high school graduation–" Mom can't go on. She's crying again.

Bess puts an arm around her. "Oh, honey, if it means that much to you, take a sport coat down to the funeral home and see if that fella will put it on him."

"Thank you," Mom says.

They exit toward Uncle Buster's bedroom, and I sit down at the table. "Hi, Aunt Bertie."

"Hmm," she says, mouth full of chicken.

"Chicken looks good," I say.

"Mm-hm," she nods.

Not wanting to come between this woman and her food, I excuse myself. "I think I'll go check on my mom."

I walk down the hall and stop by the old wooden shelves full of books. Uncle Buster loved Westerns. There's an entire collection of Louis L'Amour paperbacks with wrinkled spines. I scan the titles and pull out a book called *The Haunted Mesa.* Flip it over. Skim the back cover. Maybe I'll hang onto this one and read it. I'll ask Mom if that's okay.

I ease on down the hall and step inside the bedroom. Mom and Aunt Bess stand by the bed, arms crossed, faces severe, staring down at three sport coats: navy, black, and gray. It seems to be an insurmountable task to decide which would look best with the white shirt and blue jeans Uncle Buster's body is currently wearing.

Looking around, I'm a little stunned. The room is immaculate. In my memory, this place was full of stacks. Stacks of yellowing newspapers, stacks of dusty books, stacks of old documents and unwanted mail. Stacks on the floor, on the dresser, on the chest of drawers. Now, there's not a piece of paper or a book in sight. Every surface is clean except for a pink suitcase in the corner and a matching overnight case on the dresser.

"Aunt Bess, thank you for understanding," Mom says. "With the viewing tonight and funeral tomorrow, I just feel like I've come in on the tail end of things."

*Viewing tonight? Did I hear that correctly? What is a viewing, and will it be over in time for us to be back in the motel by 7:59?*

"You just take that on to the funeral home," Bess says. "And don't worry about a thing. We've got it all under control."

My mind is reeling and I want to protest, but I know this isn't the time. Bess puts her arm around Mom and they walk out together, Mom cradling the gray sport coat lovingly in her arms. They pass by me like I'm invisible.

Still stunned, I turn to follow. But on my way out, I catch a glimpse of a small stack of papers sticking out from under the pink overnight case on the dresser. Curious, I hang back and slide the papers out far enough to read the words MOUNTAIN-AIRE HOMES. It's a stack of flyers. Same ad. Same cheesy picture.

Pulse rising, I tuck this tidbit of information away to figure out later and catch up with Mom. She's back in the kitchen, nodding hypnotically while the aunts fill her in on the funeral plans. A black limousine will come to the house. Of course, Mom and I can join them, they tell her. Bertie's son, Arnie, will be officiating because he's an ordained minister, even though he hasn't found the right church yet. The service will be at the Laurel Chapel. It's nondenominational.

Mom looks confused. "But when Uncle Buster went to church – which I know wasn't often – he attended the Methodist church in town."

"Oh honey," Bess says, "I don't think it matters. This chapel is closer and they let you use your own minister."

Bertie chimes in. "We know Buster would've wanted to hear Arnie preach."

"Okay..." Mom says, seeming unconvinced. But she's not looking at the aunts. She's staring past them into the living room.

"Eva..." Bertie waves a hand in front of Mom's face and breaks her trance.

"Oh, yes, well, we'd better get going," Mom says. She heads for the side door since the garage is still open and puts her hand on the doorknob. She stops, turns. "One more thing," she says. "I understand that Uncle Buster had a will. Is that right?"

Bess raises her eyebrows and smiles. "Well, that would be the wise thing, but we don't have knowledge of one. Do you?"

"That's strange," Mom says. "Barney over at the funeral home told me there was a will that named you as executrix."

Bess smiles and shakes her head. "Oh honey, that man wouldn't let us plan the funeral without some kind of paperwork. I finally convinced him I had a copy of a will back at the house. He's still waiting to see it. I was hoping you might know where one was."

"No," Mom says. "You know Uncle Buster. He kept all of his papers in stacks. Stacks in the bedroom, stacks on the kitchen table, even a stack in his glove compartment. He had a very unorthodox filing system."

Bess laughs. "That's our Buster," she says, and pulls a tissue from her pocket to dab her watery eyes.

Mom tries to smile, but her bottom lip quivers. She tilts her head to the side. "Thanks, Aunt Bess," she says, and then she opens the door.

I follow her silently through the garage. I want to tell her about the blueberry bushes and the flyers, but between the twittering of songbirds and the rumbling of farm equipment in the background, I decide to wait until we're in the car.

Mom hangs the gray sport coat in the back and then climbs in. Once our doors are shut, she says, "Something just doesn't seem right. Sam, did you notice the chair? Uncle Buster's favorite yellow chair? In all the shock last night I guess I didn't notice that it's covered with a quilt, tucked in tight on all sides. Now, why would they do that?"

I shrug, not sure what to make of this decorating update. I have some actual not-right-things of my own to share. Mom starts the car and I'm just about to say something, but that's when she freezes. She's looking in the rear-view mirror. Mouth open, eyes squinted, forehead wrinkled.

I turn around to see what has suddenly transfixed her. In the distance, across the fields of shrubs and young trees, I see Jud Waverly. He's driving Uncle Buster's tractor and hauling some wide, flat attachment behind it. Gruntin' Jud is pulling down all the vegetation and systematically creating a smooth pasture.

Mom shakes her head, steps on the gas, and says, "Something is definitely not right."

# Seven

We're back at the funeral home with Barney, and he's looking a little flustered. Apparently, putting a sport coat on the deceased is not going to be convenient at this point.

"Please," Mom begs, "it's important to me."

Barney sighs. "It was just very difficult to get the sleeves over his hands without making a mess. We finally tucked his hands at his sides..."

Mom tilts her head. "I don't understand."

"It's just that we used a lot of make-up on his hands, but it was too difficult to cover the..." Barney searches for words.

"The what?!" Mom raises her voice.

"The wounds on his hands," Barney says.

"Why would he have wounds on his hands?" Mom asks. This conversation is getting very interesting.

"Ma'am, I'm not sure of the answer. His sister explained that he may have crawled, or struggled to stand, or perhaps was writhing on the floor—"

"Enough!" Mom holds up the stop-talking-palm and silences Barney. "Just please put him in the sport coat."

She pivots and makes a beeline for the door. And I'm thinking, *this woman knows how to make an exit.*

We're back at the Mountaineer Inn before she says another word. "I don't get it, Sam. Maybe they're just trying to protect me. But I'm not so sure..." Her voice trails off.

"Not so sure of what?" I ask her.

"I'm just not completely convinced it was a heart attack. I mean, yes, Uncle Buster had high blood pressure, and he wasn't good about taking his medicine, but how can we be sure?" She seems to deflate and sinks onto the bed.

I break the silence with the news about the blueberry bushes. She's intrigued. Then I mention dangerous-dude Carl and the skinny-tie guy. Her wheels are turning. This is the kind of stuff she can run with. And here she goes...

"Do you think Carl could have done something? Was there a fight? That would explain the hands. We don't know of any signs of a break-in, but Aunt Bess said she called and *asked* Carl to break in to see if Uncle Buster was okay."

I hop on this runaway train. "So, what if Carl came over and started an argument? He's a neighbor, so Uncle Buster would have let him in. The argument starts. Things get heated. Pretty soon Carl is throwing punches and Uncle Buster is trying to defend himself."

Mom thinks for a minute. "But they said he vomited. I don't think that's consistent with a fight." She pounds the mattress with her fist. "There should have been an autopsy. I'm going to talk to my aunts about that."

"Good idea." And just like that, we have a plan.

The viewing starts at 6:00, but we decide it's best to show up a little early. I get decked out in a dress shirt, khakis, belt, loafers...the whole nine yards. Mom wears a navy blue dress, pink sweater, and pearls. Watch out, Ashe County. Looks like the preppies have come to town.

We grab a drive-through dinner, and Mom apologizes profusely. She promises home-cooked meals for a solid month once we're back in Jacksonville. I'm chewing, so I can't tell her I'm good with fast food. No complaints here.

We pull into the funeral home parking lot and stuff our trash into one bag. Mom looks around for a garbage can so the Jeep won't smell like fries when we return. We spot one at the corner of the building and hurry toward it. But once we're there, we're not in such a hurry anymore. As a matter of fact, we both freeze because from the corner, we see what's parked under the canopy on the side of the Ashe County Funeral Home. *BYE-BESS* has already arrived.

"This is good," Mom says, like she's convincing herself. "It'll give me a chance to talk with my aunts about an autopsy before guests arrive." And then she's off.

Once again, I'm speed-walking to keep up with her. We barrel through the double-door entrance and follow the "Friends of Buster Munroe This Way" sign to find the room. Flower arrangements are crammed on both ends of the casket, overpowering the small space with their fragrance. A heavy gold curtain forms a dusty backdrop, and at the foot end of the casket, a rickety little table holds a large framed photograph. It's a picture of Uncle Buster and Aunt Bess sitting in a restaurant booth. She's all smiles, but his usual poker-face shows a hint of irritation, and his eyes are caught in mid-blink. There are tons of family photographs hanging on the walls in his house -- and she had to bring this one?

41

Mom pays no attention to any of these details. Her teary eyes are focused on her uncle. She walks numbly, step by slow, methodical step, until she reaches the casket. The aunts are already there, leaning on one another and swaying side to side.

"Oh Eva," Bess says, "he looks so handsome in his sport coat. You made a good call, dear."

Mom leans her head on Bess's shoulder.

"He loved you so much," Bertie says to Mom.

"And I loved him," Mom replies. I'm not sure the timing is right, but she takes this opening to launch her mission. "And because I loved him, I want to ask for something."

The aunts suddenly get taller. Their faces tense up. Hands drop to their sides.

"I think we should have an autopsy performed."

"Oh honey," Bess sighs. She's breathing again, and blood returns to her face. "We can't do that. People will be here any minute, and the funeral is already set for tomorrow morning."

"Can't we postpone it?" Mom asks. "I think this is important."

Bertie's turn. "Sweetheart, you've already been through so much, losing your parents like you did. It's difficult to accept the passing of someone you love, but Uncle Buster's heart just gave out."

"You know, I did everything I could to help him," Bess adds, dabbing tears with a tissue. "I came down as often as I could. I reminded him to take his medicine, and when I saw him looking poorly and sluggish, I set up the Meals on Wheels to be sure he was eating."

"I know," Mom concedes. She sounds weak.

Bertie continues. "Bess made sure he always had food to eat. She even told that delivery woman that if he didn't answer the door, she was to just leave the meal on the porch. He'd be back soon enough to get it."

"Is that safe? Wouldn't the food spoil?" Mom asks. "Are they even allowed to do that?"

"Well, they're not supposed to leave the meal," Bess answers, patting Mom's hand. "But I wanted to be sure he had some food. He was lookin' more and more feeble ever since he retired. His porch was in the shade. It was fine."

"I understand..." Mom's crying again.

"Eva, honey," Bertie says gently, "don't let your imagination get carried away. Like Bess said, Buster's heart just gave out. That ol' rascal never would take his medicine like he was supposed to."

Mom nods and falls into a group hug. It's 6:00, and guests are arriving. The three women peel themselves apart from their embrace and begin to greet the mourners as they trickle in.

The first one there is Carl Leibowitz, wearing a tweed jacket and his customary scowl. Behind him are three church-lady types with purses dangling from their elbows. They go straight for Mom and the aunts. So I figure the polite thing to do is greet Carl.

"Hello, I'm Sam Parsons, Buster's great-nephew." I hold out my hand. He looks at it before he shakes it.

"Hmm," he mumbles. "Your great-uncle was a good man."

As Carl and I stand side by side in awkward silence, we hear the aunts recounting their estimation of Uncle Buster's death scenario. The doily, the vomit, the Salisbury steak, right over left, the pocket change. Wait, I don't remember pocket change. Bess says there was 85 cents on the floor.

"Three quarters and two nickels," Bertie adds.

They shake their heads in sorrowful solidarity.

"When do you think he passed?" one of the church ladies asks.

"Must've been Monday," Bertie says. "Jud Waverly's sure he saw Buster alive on Sunday."

"But I thought you said no one had seen him for a couple of weeks," another church lady interjects.

Mom's forehead wrinkles. She's obviously intrigued by this new detail and waits for a response.

Bess clears her throat. "We said we couldn't get ahold of Buster for two weeks," she clarifies. "But Jud was coming around the curve late Sunday, on his way up to Laurel Chapel for the evenin' service. Just as he passed Buster's mailbox, he remembers looking up and seeing him through the picture window."

"Oh," the church ladies say in unison, all nodding.

But then Carl's face darkens. He turns to me and says one word. "Impossible."

Okay Carl, I'll play this game. "What's impossible?" I ask.

"You can't see Buster's front window from the road. Even if you dare to look up from that curve, you see the driveway, the side of the hill, maybe even the roof and chimney. But you can't see that window behind all those blueberry bushes."

Carl shakes his head, pays his respects to the body in the casket, and then walks out. But he doesn't leave the building. Instead, he sits down next to shadow-lady June in the lobby, and they huddle together in hushed conversation. *So they know each other. Interesting.*

At least twenty other people have filed in at this point. I catch mom's attention and let her know I need a little air. Really, I want to stroll through the lobby and attempt some eavesdropping.

I stop in a little alcove, at a table filled with pamphlets. I pretend to be deeply interested in *Planning Your Funeral* and *Ralph's Limousine Rentals*, but from the corner of my eye I'm making observations.

From where I'm standing, I can't see their faces. But I have a good view of their hands. June still has dirt under her fingernails, and on her fingers too, for that matter. Maybe they're just stained that way. Carl's hands are clenched in fists, but I'm able to notice something very interesting. He has a white loop on his left ring finger, like an un-tanned spot where a wedding band used to be. I'm curious.

I can't hear what they're saying, so as I make my way to the door, I veer toward them. No luck. They stop talking and make a move toward the "Friends of Buster Munroe This Way" sign. I continue on outside. I don't want to arouse suspicion.

Even though it's a little hazy outside, I have no problem spotting June's truck. I know it by the magnetic Meals on Wheels sign still stuck to the driver's side door. I move closer. Take a look around. A quick glance through the window reveals a couple of pieces of unopened mail addressed to June Halstrap. I make a mental note of her last name but keep the casual forward progress going.

That's when I notice something that stops me in my tracks. Black dirt is spilled all over the bed of June's pick-up. And while I don't know plants all that well, I see a few familiar-looking leaves scattered in the bed. I scan the area. Make sure no one is watching. Then I climb up on June's bumper and reach into the bed. I grab one of the leaves and tuck it in my pocket. I'll have to confirm later, but I'm almost certain it's from a blueberry bush.

My heart is racing as I hop off the bumper. I look around once more. And then my heart stops. There's a big brown pick-up parked in the grass at the front corner of the lot. I hadn't noticed it before, but I can make out the silhouette of a large person sitting in the driver's seat. Suddenly, the silhouette turns and a familiar face is illuminated by shards of sunlight straining through foreboding clouds. The eyes now staring directly at me belong to none other than Jud Waverly.

Heart pounding, I quick-step toward the front door of the funeral home. As soon as my hand grips the door knob, I hear an engine crank. I turn to watch the big brown pick-up pull out onto the highway.

# Eight

We're back in our motel room by 8:10. Mom apologizes. Says it's the best she could do. I tell her it's fine. She decides to take a hot shower and I hop on the Wi-Fi.

I start streaming the draft before responding to the six missed messages from Oscar. The commentators are still yammering ahead of the first pick, and I start to text Oscar, but suddenly talk turns to my Jags.

Talking head #1: "The Jaguars have one major goal to accomplish if they want to be successful. They need to strengthen their offense." *Yeah, everybody knows that.*

Talking head #2: "Heisman-trophy-winning quarterback Marshall Mills is the kind of aggressive playmaker they need, but they can dream on."

Talking head #3: "He's sure to be gone way ahead of their pick." *As I have predicted.*

Sam

Sam

Sam

Oscar's getting impatient.

I'm here. I'm watching.

UR alive!

48

Talking head #1 says, "I think the Jags will try to snag Rimington Trophy winner Carlos Mendez. A stand-out center could be the ticket to strengthening that O-line."

Oscar can't resist commenting.

> U hear that?

> I'm sticking with Sumi. We need a wide receiver. What about Joey?

> RB Lamar Sapp.

> Running back? No way.

Draft coverage cuts to the stage. The NFL Commissioner stands at the mic in executive fashion and announces the first pick. "The New York Jets select quarterback Marshall Mills!"

The scene cuts to what looks like a community center filled with friends and family of the Heisman-winning QB. They jump up and down as he dons a Jets cap. His mother cries and hugs him, his father high fives everyone within reach, and I sigh. They should have gone with Mendez. Their mistake.

The players-turned-commentators congratulate themselves and begin arguing about the next pick. As they talk, these guys wave their hands around in grand gestures, making sure everybody sees their Super Bowl rings.

Rings. That sends my mind on a detour. His finger-tan line indicates that Carl Leibowitz used to be married. *So where's his wife now? Hmm.* I decide to take a little draft break and search up Carl Leibowitz.

There's a Carl Leibowitz who's an attorney in Michigan, age
42. *Too young.* Another one is 85 and lives in Florida. *Too old.*
Obituary for a Carl Leibowitz. *Definitely not him.* Wait a minute.
Carlton A. Leibowitz, from McKeesport, Pennsylvania. He's
listed in The Pittsburgh Tribune-Review as a survivor in the
obituary of Ellen Schwartz Leibowitz. *This has got to be him.*

I find a link to a guest book and read messages people left
for the deceased. She was a teacher. History. Sounds like high
school. Looks like they didn't have children. No indication of
how she died. Just says she died peacefully at home. Exactly
eighteen months ago.

A little more digging shows that the same Carl Leibowitz,
age 66, sold his home in Pennsylvania shortly after that and
bought property in Ashe County, North Carolina. *Bingo.*
*Definitely him. So how did his wife die? And what brought Carl to
Ashe County?*

O! UR burned!

Oscar's message interrupts my train of thought. I flip back to
draft coverage and see wide receiver Sumi pumping his fist in a
Raiders jersey. People are cheering, more commentary, and I
return to multi-tasking.

*What about June,* I'm wondering. *How do they know each other?*
So I run a search for June Halstrap. Seems to be a pretty popular
name in Great Britain. It takes a while, but I finally find a
feature on Marlin Halstrap in the senior section of the Ashe
County Register. Retired farmer. Widowed. Cared for by his
daughter, June. And that's the end of the road for shadow lady.

The bathroom door opens, and steam pours out. Mom materializes in the cloud, her pink pajamas and fuzzy slippers looking oddly out of place at the Mountaineer Inn. "Ah," she sighs, "I hope I didn't use all the hot water, but I sure do feel better." She sits on the side of her bed. "So, has your team gotten to pick a new player?"

I look up from my phone. "What?" *Wait, the draft. I forgot all about it.* "You wouldn't believe it," I say. "This thing is full of surprises."

Mom laughs and shakes her head, totally not intending to dig any deeper. She picks up her phone, starts checking emails.

"Mom," I interrupt. "What exactly do we know about Carl Leibowitz?"

"Carl?" Mom puts her phone down. Stares at the wall as if she'll find an answer there. "I don't guess we know a lot. He moved up here a little over a year ago. Keeps to himself mostly. Uncle Buster knew him, but I don't know how well."

"Ever hear of a Mrs. Leibowitz?" I'm baiting the hook here.

"No, just Carl. He lives alone."

"What if I told you there once was a Mrs. Carl Leibowitz? She died at home in McKeesport, Pennsylvania 18 months ago. The obituary doesn't say *how* she died. But why would the guy leave his home in Pennsylvania and move to Ashe County, North Carolina, where he doesn't know a soul?"

I ignore the successive buzz of texts from Oscar as Mom scoots to the edge of the bed. "Sam, how do you know all this?"

"I did a little searching. Because it's odd, don't you think?"

51

"Yes, but we can't jump to conclusions."

Classic. The queen of conspiracy theories is telling *me* not to jump to conclusions. "I'm not suggesting anything. I'm just saying we don't know much about him, and it all seems a little strange."

"You're right," she agrees. "It does seem odd." She's taking the bait, so I consider it an invitation to continue.

"And while I was digging, I found out June's not married. She lives with her elderly father."

"She seems sad." Mom's drifting off in thought, and I need to reel her back in. I never got to tell her about the loose dirt and missing blueberry bushes, so I break the news now. Her mouth drops open and she stares at me in disbelief.

"You noticed the plants?"

"Mom, this is real," I tell her. "When we go back up to the house, check it out." She grins, like I'm being cute or something. Time to produce some evidence.

"And check *this* out." I show her the leaf. "Doesn't this look like it came from a blueberry bush?"

"Well, yes, I think so." She wrinkles her brow.

"I found it in a pile of loose dirt in the bed of June Halstrap's pick-up."

"Sam, what were you doing in the back of her truck?!" *Oops. I hadn't counted on this reaction.*

"I went for a walk, to get some air. I just happened to notice and thought it was strange, with the bushes missing and all, so I reached in and picked up a leaf." She calms down, so I ask the obvious. "Do you think June could've been in on this? She definitely had access to his food."

"My biggest concern about his food," Mom says, "is that it would sometimes sit out on the porch. Poor Uncle Buster could have succumbed to food poisoning."

"So no autopsy?" I ask her. "Are you okay with that?"

"Oh, Sam," she says, "I can let my mind get so carried away. We can't postpone the funeral. It's all planned." She waves her hand dismissively, like she's swatting at gnats. "And you and I need to get back home. We've been away long enough."

I go ahead and tell her about Jud Waverly lurking in the funeral home parking lot, and that seems to wake her up.

"I never trusted those Waverly brothers," she says. "And neither did your Uncle Buster. Frank was okay, I guess, just a little self-important. Apparently, Jud and Bess were an item back in the day, but that ended when Jud found out he wasn't her only beau."

"If you ask me," I say, "it looks like they've rekindled the old flame. Did you see that hug in the garage?"

"Sam, he was consoling her." Mom sighs, exasperated. "Please, let's not make assumptions or start any rumors." She flops down on the bed, but her eyes are open, staring at the ceiling. I've given her plenty of material, and the wheels are turning.

> Sapp to Jags! Joey is
> killing this thing!

I've successfully ignored Oscar's texts up to this point, but I go ahead and toss him a line.

> Looks like I'm out
> twenty bucks.

My phone returns to streaming draft coverage, but my mind is barreling ahead on a different track. I don't know who, I don't know why, and I don't know how, but I'm convinced that *somebody* murdered Uncle Buster. And I'm not about to let them get away with it.

# Nine

The limo is scheduled to arrive at Uncle Buster's place at 10:00, so we wake up early, get dressed, and stop at the Four Square Diner for breakfast. The gang's all there: Fanny, the short-order cook, even June. She must be a regular.

Mom and I snag our same booth from yesterday. I order the pancake special, and she gets oatmeal with fresh blueberries and cream on the side. Again. I guess we're regulars, too.

June's not staring at us this time. She seems gloomy, resigned...perhaps remorseful? I whisper to Mom, "Are you sure June didn't have something to do with this?"

Mom leans in, whispers back. "Sam, she's lonely, sad even. But she's not a criminal. And blueberries are hardly a motive. Uncle Buster shared them with anyone who asked. If she had wanted her own blueberry bushes, he would have been more than happy to root some plants for her."

"Okay," I murmur between bites of pancake. "But what about Carl? He's an angry dude. And what's he doing here anyway?"

"That remains a mystery," Mom says. "But again, there's no motive. I can't imagine a fight. Uncle Buster saw the best in everyone. Even Carl." The tears are starting. I figure I should change the subject.

"So, the Jags went for an offensive lineman in the first round. I guess the strategy is to keep the QB and try to strengthen his protection."

"That's nice," she answers. I know she doesn't care, but at least she's not crying. I figure I'll lay off the conspiracy theories. For now. I look around the diner, trying to generate another topic of conversation. That's when the door opens, and things get interesting. It's the skinny-tie guy.

Instead of taking a seat, he struts right up to the register. Asks Fanny for a cup of coffee to go. "And can I get that with coconut milk and agave?" he asks. I almost spit out a mouthful of orange juice. Does this guy realize where he is?

Fanny's hand is on her hip. "No, but I can give you some cream and sugar," she says, not the slightest hint of hospitality in her voice. I notice June is glaring at the guy and shaking her head. The short-order cook is frozen like a statue, arms crossed, frowning.

"Uh, yeah, I'll just take it black," the guy says. "And maybe some kind of to-go food item?"

Fanny glances back at the cook. He breaks his statue pose and shrugs. Then, oddly, Fanny's eyes dart over to June, as if she's waiting for a go-ahead from the shadow lady before she answers the guy. Finally, she looks him in the eye and says, "Blueberry muffin?"

"Sure."

Fanny turns to the counter behind her and pulls a huge blueberry muffin out of a plastic container. It's something I hadn't noticed until now. Honestly, I don't even remember seeing blueberry muffins on the menu.

I'm feeling a little confused, but everything else is settling back to normal. June is eating quietly, the short-order cook is busy in the kitchen, and Fanny rings up the to-go order. Skinny-tie guy leaves, and the air feels instantly lighter.

"Well, I don't know what all that was about," Mom says. So she noticed it, too. "But we should settle up and get moving." We pay Fanny up at the register and Mom gives her a generous tip. Of course, there's no reaction from Fanny.

We head up to Uncle Buster's, and as we reach the sharp curve at Route 6, Box 322, I remind Mom of the blueberry bushes. We roll the windows down and maneuver slowly up the rocky driveway. "I see what you mean," Mom says. "It's like they've been thinned out." The car rolls to a stop and we just sit there, quietly, like we're trying to listen for something we aren't able to hear. April breezes and bird songs meander through our emptiness.

Thanks to gruntin' Jud Waverly, the once-familiar tall grasses, scrub bushes, and young trees have all been erased. It's like we're in the end zone, looking across a long, flat football field. In the distance, tall trees stand guard where the forest begins. We can hear the repetitive *rat-a-tat-tat* rhythm of a woodpecker echoing across the hollow space.

But it's hard to focus on the distance because of the distractions all around us. It's like a shrill, high-pitched argument is being waged. Little gray birds are everywhere. They look like somebody took bright yellow paint and swashed it across the tops of their heads and wings. Their eyes wear dark masks, and beneath their long, sharp beaks, black feathers funnel themselves to a point, resembling tufts of hair. "What's up with all the little Blackbeards?" I ask.

"Blackbeards?"

"These birds – they're everywhere! Look at the black feathers under their beaks. Doesn't that look like a beard?"

"Oh!" Mom laughs. "Songbirds have always loved this place," she says. We sit motionless, mesmerized, watching the little blackbeards shout, sing, and chase each other in a game of aerial tag.

Our bird show is interrupted when the front door opens and Aunt Bertie steps out onto the porch. The winged entertainers scatter as her sizable presence emerges in all black – black dress, black stockings, black shoes, hat, and gloves. *Do women even wear gloves anymore?*

"Yoo-hoo! Eva!" she calls, waving a gloved hand. "You can't park there! The limo will need to get all the way up the drive so it can turn around. It's quite long, you know!"

Mom nods and waves back. "Oh yes!" she calls. "We're just admiring the birds!"

"Uh-huh," Bertie says, but she looks confused. Mom swings wide around *BYE-BESS* and pulls in on the far side, under a shady red maple.

The garage door is closed, so we stroll around and enter through the front door. Mom stops without warning, and I almost bump into her. At first I think she's letting her eyes adjust, but then I notice a 30-something character sitting in

Uncle Buster's quilt-covered chair. Although I haven't seen him in years, the protruding Adam's apple, mass of curly brown hair, and grayish-blue eyes tell me right away it's Bertie's son, Arnie. But what is he doing sitting in Uncle Buster's chair? Seems like the reverend should be a little more reverent about something so sacred.

He stands and sticks his hand out. "Good to see you, Cousin Eva."

"Oh, Arnie," Mom says, "you can do better than that." She reaches out and gives him an awkward hug.

"Arnie is an ordained pastor, did you know that?" Bertie interjects.

"Yes," Mom says politely. "You mentioned that." *Only about fifteen times.*

"I'm honored to officiate at the funeral," he says.

"Buster would be so proud," Bertie proclaims, and then the waterworks are unleashed. Arnie consoles his mother, and Mom and I leave them to each other. We walk into the kitchen, and I'm wondering where Bess is. I turn to ask Mom, but she's revolving in a slow circle, studying the walls with growing distress.

Bess suddenly appears at the bedroom door and swaggers toward the kitchen. She's wearing long black pants with wide legs that sway back and forth as she walks. A flowing black shirt hangs over her like a tent. Her sleeves flare out at the bottom and remind me of tolling bells. But believe it or not, Bess is not the strangest thing I see. As she walks down the hallway, she's not passing any Louis L'Amour books. The hallway is empty. All the old Westerns are gone, along with the shelves that housed them.

As soon as Bess steps into the kitchen she says, "Hello, E—" but Mom cuts her off.

"Where are all the pictures?" she asks. Then I see it. Uncle Buster's walls, once filled with old family photos, are empty. Tiny nails and rectangles of un-faded yellow paint remain like echoes in the void.

"Oh, sweetheart," Bess says gently. "They needed to be cleaned. And preserved. I'm going to put them all in albums. And I'll get copies made of any I think you might want. I'll send them to you."

"Oh, okay..." Mom says. I get the feeling there's more she wants to say, but she just stands there, frozen.

Arnie is now pacing back and forth feverishly in the living room, papers in hand. His free arm keeps waving wildly as he walks, his face is contorting into all kinds of expressions, and his mouth is moving, but no sound is coming out. Probably rehearsing his eulogy.

Finally, Mom thinks of something to say. "Will Jud be joining us this morning?" she asks. *Way to break the ice, Mom.*

Bess just smiles and tilts her head to one side. "No, the limo is for family only. Jud'll be meeting us at the Laurel Chapel.

"Oh, well he's starting to seem like family, what with all the work he's doing around here," Mom says. "One might conclude he's preparing to move in." *We don't want to make assumptions or start rumors, but hey, she's pursuing this thing.*

"He's just an old friend," Bess answers, and immediately, a sound pops out of Bertie – *is it a giggle or a hiccup?*

I have a feeling this conversation could get pretty intense, but it's brought to an abrupt end by a streak of sunlight glinting off the side of a long, black limousine pulling up the driveway.

# Ten

The limo has two rows of seating behind the driver's clear glass panel. *Is it soundproof?* There's a sign above the glass that says "Ralph's Limousine Service" with a toll-free phone number. Just like on the pamphlet from the funeral home.

Arnie squeezes in the back with the aunts, leaving Mom and me alone in the middle seat. We can't see the trio behind us, but we can definitely hear them. The aunts immediately squirm, and Bess asks Arnie to "scooch" over. I sense that their intent was for him to sit with us, but Arnie's not one to pick up on subtle hints.

Laurel Chapel is up the mountain from Uncle Buster's place, so we take a left at the mailbox and climb the side of the curve we don't usually travel. Thick shrubs and thin trees line the roadside for about fifty to a hundred yards on either side. Beyond that, the forest begins to climb toward the surrounding mountains. For the first time, I realize how beautiful, and truly peaceful, this place really is. But the peace is interrupted by hushed voices behind us.

It's not Arnie doing the talking. He's seated behind Mom, so if I casually turn my head, I can see him from the corner of my eye. He's staring out the window. Probably still rehearsing in his mind. But the aunts are whispering back and forth.

"I never realized how many mobile homes were back up in here," Bertie says. "And some of them are covered with rust." She's unfiltered like that, so I figure it's her not-so-tactful way of expressing compassion for families living in rusty mountain trailers.

But then Bess responds with, "It really drives the property value down. The county shouldn't allow it." *Ouch. Harsh.* I remind myself that she's a real estate agent. I guess it's just the way she thinks. However, their conversation continues and makes me increasingly uncomfortable.

"What can be done?" Bertie asks, a little too loudly.

Bess adjusts her volume to barely audible, but the acoustics in this limo are awesome. "Well, nothing right now," she whispers. "But it may not matter. There's not a lot of this mess until you round the curve. Anyone being shown the property would be coming up from town. They won't see this side of it."

*Anyone being shown the property? Are they talking about Uncle Buster's place?* I haven't realized until now that Mom must be listening, too. She cuts her eyes at me and we share a moment of silent shock.

All conversation comes to a halt when the limo slows and swings wide into a rocky clearing in front of Laurel Chapel. It's a small cinder-block building surrounded by trees. Windows along each side and double doors on the front are all wide open. A white steeple is mounted above the entrance, and for lack of a formal parking lot, cars are arranged haphazardly in patches of shade.

The limo pulls up in front of the church, and the driver – Ralph, I'm guessing – opens the door for us. Mom and I crawl out and go stand under the archway that's holding up the steeple. The aunts make a slower exit. Bess reaches her hand out, and Ralph takes the cue. He assists her – pulls her, really – out of the back seat. Same procedure for Bertie, but it takes a little more effort on Ralph's part.

Ralph reflexively backs away as Arnie scrambles out of the limo and hurries around to escort the aunts, stepping in between them so they can each take an elbow.

The trio strides slowly, the ladies in black wearing solemn expressions but holding their heads high. Between them, Arnie is plagued by coils of unkempt hair that keep falling in his face. Without a free hand, he's trying to blow upward gusts of breath toward his forehead to reposition his mane.

Once inside, we're escorted to the front row of the chapel by none other than the Waverly brothers. Gruntin' Jud is wearing a snug black suit and scuffed brown cowboy boots. His brother, Sheriff Frank Waverly, is easily recognizable in his dress uniform, a shiny star pinned to the front of one side of his dark jacket and a brass name tag pinned to the other. Each sleeve bears a patch that says: Sheriff, Ashe County. Just in case there's any doubt, I guess.

I enter the pew first, followed by Mom, Aunt Bertie, and finally Aunt Bess. As we take our seats, Frank distributes paper fans and says, "We couldn't arrange to have the AC turned on, so you might need these."

Then the Waverly brothers lead Arnie up to the pulpit, and they sit – Frank on the piano bench and Jud on a stool nearby. *Seriously?*

During the ten or so minutes before the service begins, I scan the funeral bulletin. There's a fuzzy picture of Uncle Buster on the front, along with his name and dates of birth and death. I hadn't realized they'd settled on an official date of death, but it looks like they're sticking with Monday.

Mom's reading it, too, but she's already turned to the inside. She leans over and whispers to me, "They're really going to sing 'How Great Thou Art?' at Uncle Buster's funeral? That was his least favorite hymn. He thought it was way too dramatic. Used to joke about it."

I shrug. "Maybe he'll think it's funny."

Mom squeezes my hand, and for the first time in a while, she smiles. Really smiles.

Suddenly, Frank hits a chord on the piano and knocks the smile off Mom's face. The church is instantly quiet. Jud walks up to the pulpit and pulls the microphone out of its stand.

"Oh Lord, my God..." he sings, "when I, in awesome wonder...." Cue vibrato. Uncle Buster thought this hymn was too dramatic? I wonder if he'd ever heard Jud sing it. Because Gruntin' Jud Waverly is taking the drama to an extreme.

Jud's face looks pained. The veins on his neck bulge. One hand is confined by the mic, but the other one looks like it's squeezing an invisible stress ball. His voice pays little attention to the key and even less attention to the tempo. To Frank's credit, he continually adjusts the chords to keep up. The hymn ends on a high note that Jud holds until he's blue in the face.

I lift my hands to clap, not to encourage Jud, but just to be polite. I immediately realize this isn't a clapping occasion. A few "Amens" echo around the chapel. Frank returns to the piano bench, but Jud comes down and squeezes in next to Aunt Bess. And then Arnie, stretching to his full height and generating his most serious facial expression, steps up to the pulpit.

"Friends of Butter Munroe," he begins, "I- I- mean *Buster* Munroe." I use every ounce of self-control to stifle a laugh while sweat beads up on Arnie's forehead. "We gather here today to remember a hard-working man." Several sighs of relief affirm Arnie as he seems to be back on track.

"And speaking of hard-working, scripture tells us that 'The soul of the sluggard desireth and hath nothing; but the soul of the diligent shall be made fat.' Well, not to say that he was fat." Arnie fumbles with his papers. "That's um, from Proverbs, chapter.... well, from Proverbs." A light breeze moves across the church, giving relief to everyone but Arnie. His trembling hands lose their grip on his sermon notes and the papers splay out in all directions.

Bertie whisper-yells from the front row, "Just talk about Buster, dear. Speak from your heart." She smiles with nervous encouragement.

Arnie nods. "Buster was my uncle. He was a simple man." He grips the sides of the podium and straightens his posture. "He worked at, uh, a hardware store, as I recall. And he um, he liked blackberries."

Aunt Bertie's head is bobbing up and down, and she's hanging on every word. Aunt Bess, on the other hand, is squirming uncomfortably. Poor Jud's just trying to stay awake. Coughs, squirms, and creaking pews fill the chapel as Arnie continues.

"But now, friends, he has moved on. Change has come to Buster, just as change will come to the place he once called home."

Mom and I simultaneously turn to look at Aunt Bess, who's making emphatic gestures aimed at getting Arnie to wrap it up. Now. But again, Arnie's not good with hints, so he keeps on talking. "The many little cabins that will line the hillside will represent the many memories we hold dear." Mom stiffens and frowns, and I can feel the heat rising from her rigid frame.

Suddenly, a strong gust of wind whips through the open windows, sending Arnie's sermon notes rolling like tumbleweeds, knocking over a couple of flower arrangements, and whisking a frantic bird into the church. The little feathered frenzy flies erratically. It dive-bombs the pews and circles Arnie, who's cowering at the pulpit, hands protectively cradling his curly head. Some people yelp and duck while others swat the air with their funeral fans, trying to guide the panicky bird toward an exit.

Instinctively, Frank starts playing a calming hymn on the piano. The bird finds an open window, the mourners regain their composure, Arnie takes a seat, and the world's most awkward funeral sermon comes to an abrupt end.

At Frank's cue, Jud returns to the microphone for a slow but passionate rendition of "Amazing Grace." Actually, it's almost beautiful.

The family is escorted out of the chapel first. Bess leads the way and seems to be in a hurry. She's leaving Bertie in her dust. Bertie strolls slowly, head held high, nodding left and right to acknowledge the solemn-faced mourners. We bring up the rear, and Mom lovingly touches a few shoulders along the way.

I feel tears forming in my eyes, and I don't know whether it's sadness over the loss of Uncle Buster or regret that I didn't get to know him better. So what if he lived in the boonies and didn't have Wi-Fi? He was a really good guy, and I should have paid attention.

My mind is suddenly shaken from its melancholy as we approach the back of the church. I notice June and Carl sitting together on the last pew to my left. June is sobbing into a wadded up tissue, but Carl is wearing his familiar scowl. He glares at all of us as we pass by, and a cold chill runs down my spine.

The sun is at high noon and scorching hot, so we move toward the shady overhang of oak trees. "What's up with Arnie and all the little cabins?" I say to Mom. "Does that mean they're selling the property to Mountain-Aire Homes?"

"Oh, you can bet I'll have a conversation with my aunts this afternoon," Mom says through a sideways smile. "But for now, we will smile and thank the guests for attending. Some will want to follow us to the family cemetery, and a few may even join us at the house later." Sounds like a long time to sit on a conversation.

Arnie has joined Bertie in the shade beneath a poplar tree, but I notice that Bess is nowhere near them. She's standing by the limo, fanning herself while engaged in what appears to be a very solemn conversation with Jud Waverly. The three church ladies from the funeral home approach Bertie and try to find a way to compliment Arnie.

"That was so..." begins one of them. But she can't quite find the adjective she's looking for.

"Special." Another member of the trio finishes her sentence.

"Yes, special," the first one confirms.

The third church lady looks over at Bess and Jud. Then she leans in and speaks softly, so I attempt a little covert action to move nearer without being noticed.

"It's hard to say," I hear Bertie whisper. "But they've been spending a lot of time together, and Jud's been jumping like a rabbit to respond to her every desire."

Arnie speaks up. He seems to have found his confidence. "Mama, you don't want to gossip, now."

"Oh, it's not gossip," the third church lady declares. "We need to know the details so we know exactly what to pray for."

All the ladies nod with self-righteous assurance. They continue to whisper, but I'm feeling a need to get back into the shade. I casually step backwards, trying to reclaim my earlier position, and *bam*.

"Whoa, there, young man!" I turn to see I've backed right into Carl Leibowitz. He's holding his hands in the air. I'm frozen, but I stammer out an apology.

Carl doesn't respond. Just stares right into my eyes. But as he lowers his hands, I notice his knuckles are covered with scratches that have scabbed over and started to heal. They're not fresh scratches. Maybe a week old. My heart is pounding and my mouth goes dry.

Just then, June stumbles behind Carl and approaches Mom. She's still crying into what looks like the same wadded-up tissue. Mom hugs her and pulls a clean tissue from her purse. "Thank you for delivering the meals," she says. "That meant so much to all of us."

"I shouldn't have left the meals out when he wasn't there," June sobs. "Your aunt told me to, so I did, but do you think he could've gotten food poisoning?" June looks truly horrified. "It's all I've thought about. I hope I didn't..." Her words morph into sobs.

"No, no, no," Mom says, and hugs her again. "Please put your mind at ease. According to my aunts, Uncle Buster spilled his Salisbury steak and green peas all over the floor. He was still in the process of eating it, and the effects of food poisoning don't start until at least four hours after consuming contaminated food." Sounds like Mom did a little research.

June's face remains strained, but her tight shoulders relax a little. "Salisbury steak," she repeats. "That was his favorite. I left it on Friday..." Her voice trails off and she seems unable to generate any more words.

With all this emotion, I almost forget that the shadow looming over me is not from the oak, but from Carl. He watches June walk toward her truck. Mom notices him and says, "Mr. Leibowitz, thank you so much for coming."

I can think of a hundred different responses he could make, but I'm blown away by the words he chooses. He looks at Mom, then at me, then back at June as she cranks the engine of her pick-up. Out of the blue, the big crazy dude says, "I'm sure you people will be pleased to know there's gonna be another funeral soon."

Carl swaggers into the sunshine, but Mom and I stand motionless in the shade of the oaks and the darkness of his odd proclamation.

# Eleven

The limo winds silently past rusted mobile homes and scrubby landscape as we make our way back to the house. Tension rises from the back seat, but no words are spoken. Ralph glances in the rearview mirror, but other than that, each passenger seems to have drifted into a solitary world of contemplation. Mom stares out her window, holding my hand and holding it together as best she can.

When we pull up the driveway to Uncle Buster's house, the church ladies are there to greet us with cookies and casseroles. Skinny-tie guy is waiting on the front porch with a bag of foam cups and four jugs of sweet tea from the Piggly Wiggly.

Ralph pulls up to the garage and ushers us out of the limo and into a cloud of dust. First the middle seat, and then the back. Mom stops to stare across the newly mown field with tears in her eyes.

Bess brushes the settling dust from her flowing black tent and says, "We sure could use some rain." She looks at Mom, who deliberately avoids eye contact with the aunts but turns graciously to thank the church ladies for their casseroles.

We walk single file through the garage and into the house. Bertie helps arrange cookies and casseroles while Bess opens the front door for skinny-tie guy. Turns out his name is Kyle Jasper. And he works for Mountain-Aire Homes.

Mom tells me to help Kyle with the jugs of sweet tea, and then she makes what I can only interpret to be a power move.

She sits in Uncle Buster's quilt-covered chair. The aunts both take notice.

"Eva, dear, don't get too comfortable," Bertie says. "You'll want to come and fix yourself a plate while it's still warm." Mom doesn't respond.

Bess stands in front of her, peering through the big picture window, probably watching for Jud Waverly. Finally, in a satisfied tone, she says, "Jud must've thinned out those old blueberry bushes. It's much easier to see the road now."

Mom glances at me, and as if our shared thought suddenly materializes, June Halstrap enters through the garage carrying a foil pan filled with blueberry muffins. "Fanny sent these up," she says. "Fanny, from the diner."

"Well, now, that seems more like breakfast than dinner," Bess says in a condescending tone. Kyle and Bertie each put a muffin on their plates, and in response to Aunt Bess's rudeness, I grab a plate and two muffins.

"Mom, can I get you anything?" I ask.

"Not right now, thank you. I'm not hungry," she says through tight lips. *Bess wants rain? By the looks of Mom, a storm is brewing.*

I'm actually pretty hungry, so I get a scoop of macaroni, a little chicken salad, and some kind of hash-brown-and cheese mixture. I sit on the couch and Arnie joins me. After pausing to bless the food, he digs into his mountain of carbs.

June, Bertie, and the church ladies all sit at the kitchen table to eat. Bess fills a plate and then plants herself in a rocking chair that she tilts to face Mom. "You'll have to try this hash brown casserole, Eva. It's delicious." Then, with her mouth full of food, she yells toward the kitchen, "Hash brown casserole's delicious!"

"So what's going to happen to this place?" Mom asks.

Bess leads with an evasive response. "Now, Eva, time marches on. Things change." She can't possibly think that will put an end to the conversation.

"Really cheesy macaroni," Arnie says.

I laugh and nearly spit sweet tea through my nose.

Arnie shifts uncomfortably. "I mean, lots of cheese," he says.

"Yeah, it's good," I say, trying to recover. But then I'm glued to the unfolding drama once again.

"Eva," Bess says, "you have to understand. Buster was our brother. He knew we'd know what was best." Mom frowns and Bess stands, puts her plate on a side table, and strolls to the bedroom. Mom looks puzzled. I'm sure we all do.

Bess returns with some papers in her hands. "You were so smart to remember that Buster kept some papers in his glove compartment," she says. "We looked there and found this will. Turns out he named me as executrix after all. And he's left everything to Bertie and me."

Mom takes the will from Bess's outstretched hand. I instinctively move to her side and read over her left shoulder. His home, property, any and all monies, are left solely to his sisters, Elizabeth Munroe and Roberta Williams.

The will is signed in big, round letters by Buster Munroe and witnessed by Geraldine Waverly. *Another Waverly? Seriously? I don't remember seeing Uncle Buster's handwriting before, but honestly, the giant, loopy letters in his signature look like they were written by a middle-school girl. I'll keep that to myself.*

Mom sits up straight and speaks quietly. "What are your plans?" she asks.

Bess takes a deep breath and motions for Kyle to come near. "Well," she says, "Kyle here has been working with us to transform this old place into a beautiful vacation vista. Just think, you and your family can buy a cozy cabin. You can come and visit when you like, and rent it out the rest of the year!"

"Yes," Kyle jumps into salesman mode. "In the first phase of Mountain-Aire Homes, these 60 acres of land will be transformed into 120 homesites. You may have seen our signs."

Mom rises from the chair, no longer looking like she might cry. Her mouth tightens and her eyes grow dark. "So it's true. You're plowing down this family home-site and turning it into a tourist trap?"

That's when I notice June. She keeps her head low, dumps her paper plate in the trash, and exits the same way she entered. Nobody else seems to notice she's gone.

"We will feature 120 tastefully decorated log cabins with all the modern amenities," Kyle says. "For now, the bordering forest area will be kept intact, but as soon as rezoning goes through—"

Bess cuts him off. "We don't need to discuss all the specifics," she says. "You'll have to visit, Eva. It will be lovely."

"What do the neighbors think of this?" Mom asks.

Mom and Aunt Bess are locked in a staring contest until Mom drops the will onto the chair behind her and says, "Come on, Sam. It's time for us to leave."

I follow her through the kitchen and into the garage. Aunt Bertie is yelling after us, "Yoo-hoo! Would you like to take a plate to go?"

Mom doesn't even slow down. I follow her to the Jeep, we climb inside, and she shifts it into reverse without ever looking back. As we move swiftly down the bumpy driveway, frantic little birds shout warnings to one another, and dark clouds form overhead.

We barely pause at the mailbox, and Mom whips the Jeep out onto the road. All of a sudden, Carl Leibowitz darts out in front of us, waving his hands like a madman. Mom slams on the brakes and he directs her to pull over in the grass by his mailbox, just behind June's pick-up.

# Twelve

Mom opens her door and stands on the running board. "What's going on here?" she asks. Her voice is still tight with emotion.

Carl's face is uncharacteristically soft. He keeps his distance, but his voice is kind. "June just told me that you had no idea. I'm so sorry. I thought you were part of all this."

"Part of all what?" Mom asks.

"This whole Mountain-Aire Homes fiasco," Carl answers, throwing his hands up like that should be obvious. June stays in the background, but Carl takes a step closer to Mom and says, "Please, come on down to my house and let's talk for a bit. I won't keep you too long. I just want you to understand." He doesn't wait for an answer, but hops into the passenger side of June's pick-up.

Mom leans in and looks at me. I shrug. She falls back into the driver's seat, sighs, and follows Carl and June down a long, tree-canopied driveway. On each side of us, brushy landscape dots the gently sloping hills. A thick forest lines the background and climbs up a mountainside toward the sky.

We follow June's Meals-on-Wheels-mobile down the rambling, vegetation-lined drive until we reach a small home made of cedar siding and stone slabs. June pulls under a concrete carport attached to one side of the house and Mom parks behind her. A covered porch wraps around the house, part of it screened and part of it open. Wooden rocking chairs flank the front door and hummingbirds dart back and forth on feeders that hang from the eaves.

"Come on in," Carl says, and we follow him toward three concrete steps that lead to the side door. First Carl, then June, then Mom, and finally me. As I plant my foot on the bottom step, I look to the right and notice that out behind the carport, four blueberry bushes are standing in the sunshine. The ground around them looks fresh and loose, as if they were recently planted. I decide not to say anything to Mom right now, but I'm prepared to remain on guard and keep my eyes on the exits.

There are four wooden chairs lined with quilted seat covers at Carl's solid oak kitchen table. We each take a seat and Carl says, "I hadn't planned on company, so I apologize for not having anything to serve. I can get you some ice water if you like."

"We're fine," Mom responds. Her eyes and voice are gentle now, as if Carl's home has offered her some kind of reassurance and she wants to repay the favor. "Please, tell me about Mountain-Aire Homes."

"Well," Carl begins, "about six months ago this young fellow named Kyle showed up in town. Worked out a deal with Weston Realty to set up shop in their office." Carl pauses to sneer and shake his head before proceeding with the story. "He visited folks all along the mountain here, offering to buy up their homes and land."

June's shadowy eyes alternate between Carl and the solid oak tabletop. She nods, as if encouraging him to continue.

Carl takes a deep breath. "A few of the neighbors were interested, and Kyle gave them some sort of promissory note. The company he works for is out of Raleigh, and they want to build a big vacation development up here. Clear a bunch of land, put in a whole lot of fancy cabins. Turn this place into a tourist trap."

Mom nods. "Kyle admitted as much to me. Let me guess. They need everyone to agree to sell or it's no good, right?"

"You got it," Carl says.

That's when June chimes in. "They came to see my Pop and me. I didn't think he'd be interested, but he signed one of those notes with Kyle." She gets quiet and her eyes are suddenly fighting back tears.

Carl continues for her. "June's daddy isn't gettin' along so well, and his days are numbered." June's face drops into her hands. "Those Mountain-Aire vultures are circling. They've got him convinced that June would be better off if he sells and leaves her the money rather than the land."

"But I just love the land," June says through her tears. "I've got a big garden going, and I have my Meals on Wheels route." She gets quiet again.

Carl's face hardens and he says, "Your uncle had no interest in selling. But once that real estate agent aunt of yours caught wind of the deal, she wouldn't let up. She wanted him to sell his place and move into a retirement village up in West Virginia. Buster thought she was crazy."

Mom's shaking her head in disbelief. "He never mentioned any of this to me."

"Several weeks back, that Bess Munroe even had the nerve to suggest he should give her power of attorney over his affairs," Carl says.

Mom's eyes grow wide with shock. "Why in the world would that be necessary?"

"She claimed he was forgetting to take his medicine, wandered off sometimes, didn't answer his phone, and wouldn't be able to feed himself without the meals she arranged. She made it sound like he was losing his mind." Carl shakes his head and his face grows grim.

"Do you think she had any grounds for such a request?" Mom asks.

"No," Carl says. "Buster may have been lookin' a little peaked, but his mind was just fine."

Mom lets out a big sigh and we all sit there in silence for what seems like an eternity. Until now, I haven't noticed the *tick, tick, tick* of the analog clock on the wall behind Carl's head. I'm mesmerized watching the second hand make its slow but steady rotation.

But then I spot something more mesmerizing. Just below the clock is a wedding photo. The colors have faded some and it's slightly crooked inside its thin metal frame. The groom is obviously a much younger Carl. He's smiling from ear to ear, standing arm in arm with his petite bride. Blonde curls peek out from under her floppy hat. Her white dress is covered with lace and she holds a bouquet of yellow daisies.

Carl sees me staring. "That's my Ellen," he says, and his eyes grow warm. "We lived just outside of Pittsburgh. Ellen was a school teacher and I worked for an engineering firm in the city. But she loved these mountains."

He pauses and looks down at his hands as if they carry his story. "We spent our honeymoon over in Boone, trying to learn to ski." He chuckles. "We weren't very good at it, so we decided to go exploring instead. We drove through these back roads of Ashe County, and for some reason, my Ellen fell in love with this place. We decided this is where we'd retire." His voice is soft, and his eyes are glassy. "She wanted to grow those little mountain roses all around the house. When people asked her what else she planned to do, she'd say, 'I'll sit on the porch and watch the birds.' Ellen loved birds."

Carl swallows hard, and we're saved from utter silence by the ticking analog clock and the melody of birdsong drifting through an open kitchen window. Finally, Carl takes a deep breath and says, "She retired, and she was just waiting on me. I was determined to make it to forty years at the firm. Well, I made my forty years, but Ellen didn't live to see it. She passed away a month before I retired."

"Oh, Carl, I'm so sorry," Mom says. She reaches out and touches his elbow. "I had no idea."

"I decided to move here anyway," Carl tells us. "I planted those little wild rose bushes all around the house. They tear my hands up tryin' to pull the weeds out from under them, but I don't mind. And, of course, I sit on the porch and watch the birds. And I talk to her." His eyes well up with tears. "Buster was a good friend. He understood what it was like to be lonely."

After another awkward pause punctuated by clock ticks and birdsong, June says, "Well, I oughta get going. I've been away from Pop a little longer than I intended." She stands and lifts her chair slightly, pushing it under the table without a sound. But she doesn't go anywhere.

Finally, she lifts her eyes to meet Mom's. "Mrs. Parsons," she begins.

"Please, call me Eva," Mom says gently, encouraging June, whose shadowy eyes are once again fixed on the solid oak tabletop.

"Eva.... You may have noticed that somebody has dug up some of your uncle's blueberry bushes. I want you to know I'm to blame. I'm not exactly proud I did it, but I'm not ashamed either. Your aunts told Jud Waverly to drag 'em all down."

"Why would they do that?" Mom looks hurt but not shocked. "Uncle Buster loved his blueberry patch."

"It seems if they can go ahead and clear the land, Kyle will give them a better price," Carl says. "My understanding is that they've already finagled a deal where they'll get their cabins built at a discount because your real estate agent aunt is working for the Mountain-Aire folks."

"What kind of work?" Mom asks.

"Oh, advising, advertising, spreading the word all over the place. She's been going around town with flyers."

Mom and I exchange glances, and I know now that I wasn't crazy that first night at the Mountaineer Inn when I saw *BYE-BESS* pulling away. And Mom knows it, too.

# Thirteen

We drive back to town and Mom rolls past the Mountaineer Inn. She makes a right turn at the corner and studies the row of one-story brick storefronts. Before I have time to figure out what she's thinking, she catches me off guard with a sudden sharp left that slams me against the car door.

"Sorry, Sam. I see lights on." She parks in front of the "Law Office of Hicks and Honeycutt" and gets out.

Rubbing my shoulder and trying to figure out what's going on, I follow her up to the storefront. Before I know it, her face is pressed against the window. One hand is shielding the light above her forehead and the other is rapping on the glass.

A distinguished-looking man about Uncle Buster's age appears inside the office and points to the anything-but-subtle CLOSED sign hanging on the door. He's wearing a white polo shirt and jeans. Obviously not dressed for a day in court. *Mom, please.*

"I know!" she yells. "But this is an emergency!" *A legal emergency? Is there really such a thing?* I'm about to try to pull her away when the guy opens the door. "Thank you," she says, "it will only take a few minutes to explain."

Annoyed but obviously intrigued, he leads us to a small room practically filled by a large, shiny conference table. His jeans have a crease ironed in them, and he's wearing Italian loafers. With no socks. *Slick.*

"Please, have a seat," he tells us, "and explain the nature of your emergency. The quick version, if you don't mind."

"Thank you," Mom says breathlessly. She opens with, "I'm Eva Parsons, and this my son, Sam. And you are?"

"Byron Hicks," he answers. And that's all he says.

"Well, Mr. Hicks, my uncle was Buster Munroe. He passed away recently."

"So sorry," he says. "Please continue."

Mom takes the cue and speaks quickly. "Um, my aunts and I were trying to contact him and we couldn't reach him for several days. And then my aunts showed up and discovered that he was deceased. The sheriff was with them. They all agreed it looked like a heart attack and proceeded with funeral arrangements before I arrived."

"Mrs. Parsons," he interrupts, "I understand if your feelings are hurt—"

"It's not that," she interrupts right back and continues at warp speed. "An autopsy wasn't performed, which seems very strange to me, and the exact date of his death was not truly established. And then my aunts produced a will that leaves everything to them, and I'm just not sure it's something my uncle would have done, especially since they plan to clear the land and sell his property to the Mountain-Aire people who are going to litter the mountainside with a bunch of tacky tourist cabins, which is something he never would have wanted, I can assure you." *Whew. I think she did that all in one breath.*

Mr. Hicks leans back in his chair and inhales loudly. He taps his fingertips together and looks at the ceiling. "Now, I'm hearing two concerns here, Mrs. Parsons. First, I hear your concern that an autopsy should have been performed. Second, I hear that you have doubts as to the authenticity of this will."

"Well, yes," Mom answers, looking astounded that he's reduced her raging emotions to two simple issues.

"First, let me address the autopsy." His chair squeaks as he leans forward and looks directly at her. "If an officer of the law determines that the cause of death was consistent with a natural occurrence, a formal autopsy is not required." Mom frowns. "However," he continues, "a vial of blood is sent off for analysis. As a relative of the deceased, you should be able to submit a request for a copy of the analysis report."

"Oh..." Mom looks confused. She seems like she might be about to ask a question, but before she can gather her words, he is on to the second concern.

"Now, as for the will, I can tell you that many a family has been torn apart over the contents of a last will and testament. Feelings get hurt. Pride gets bruised. It's a difficult business."

"I just can't imagine that Uncle Buster even created a will. He wasn't one for details. But if he did, I can't imagine that he would—"

"Completely leave you out of it?" he calmly cuts her off.

"It's not that—"

"What gives you the idea this will may not be authentic? Is it signed by the deceased?" *This guy is shutting her down. I can feel it.*

"Well, yes, there is a signature, but—"

"And was the signature witnessed?"

"Yes, but—"

"Do you remember the name of the witness?"

Mom looks at me helplessly. Then the light comes on. "Yes," she tells him. "The witness was Geraldine Waverly."

Mr. Hicks smiles. "Geraldine Waverly is my partner's secretary. She's worked here for nearly thirty years. Mrs. Parsons, that will came from this office, so I assure you, it's legitimate."

"And so you would have a copy of it?" Mom asks, grasping for something, anything.

"No," he tells her. "Not unless the deceased asked us to keep a copy. Most people take it with them and put it in a place they determine to be secure and easy to find."

"Oh—" Again, shut down.

He stands. "Mrs. Parsons, I hope I have been able to put your mind at ease. Again, I'm so sorry for your loss."

"Yes, well, thank you for your time," Mom says. Her face is pale and hollow. This meeting didn't end like she had hoped. I want to do something, but I don't know what to do.

"One more thing before you go," Mr. Hicks says. He produces a paper from a narrow table pressed against the wall behind him. "Please fill out this consultation form so we can bill you by mail."

Mom looks completely deflated as she leans over the shiny table and writes her contact information on the Hicks and Honeycutt Consultation Form. Mr. Hicks stands nearby, trying to look busy while he waits for her to finish.

She stands and turns, ready to hand the form to him, but she stops. "I'm just curious," she says. "Is Geraldine Waverly any relation to Jud and Frank Waverly?"

"Well, yes," Byron answers. "She's Frank's wife. Do you know the Waverly brothers?"

"I'm acquainted," she says. "Thank you for your time, Mr. Hicks." She hands the form to him and makes a beeline for the door. Full steam ahead. No looking back. Not me, though. Something catches my eye and I pause before we exit.

There's a small waiting area just inside the front door. A brown leather couch is stretched along the cedar wall. A little end table stands beside the couch. And on that little end table, there's a nice neat stack of flyers: YOU DON'T HAVE TO BE A MILLIONAIRE TO ENJOY THE MOUNTAIN-AIRE...

# Fourteen

Mom and I sit across from each other in our regular booth at the Four Square Diner, but everything seems wrong. Fanny must have the day off, June's booth is empty, and I'm thinking this might be the last time we'll ever find ourselves in Ashe County, North Carolina. I'm guessing we won't be vacationing at a luxury Mountain-Aire cabin.

"I just don't know what to think." Mom moves the grilled chicken around on top of her salad but doesn't take a bite.

"Maybe we should talk to another lawyer," I suggest.

"No," she sighs, "there's not another law firm around here, and besides, tomorrow's Sunday. Let's focus on getting back to Jacksonville. We need to get an early start."

I'm about to take the last bite of my burger when the high school weekend-waiter returns. "Can I get you anything? Is something wrong with the salad?"

Mom cringes. "It's perfect," she says. "I'm just preoccupied. I'm sorry."

The waiter picks up my empty plate and I say, "Hey, do you know the Wi-Fi password?" I figure it's worth a try.

"Yeah, it's warbler."

"Warbler?"

"W-A-R-B-L-E-R. Some kind of bird. The owner's into birds."

"Thanks, man." Bingo. I'm on the Wi-Fi.

"No problem, dude." And he disappears into the kitchen.

Mom dives into her salad and chows down. Probably out of embarrassment. I'm streaming highlights from ESPN to catch up on the draft. I never finished watching last night's rounds. I've been a little distracted.

And Oscar's a little obsessed. He's sent a barrage of messages with so many emojis that his text thread looks like a rebus story. I want to reply, *Geez, Oscar, give it a rest*, but I'm thinking he would classify that as "harsh." Instead, I'm ignoring his messages until I can catch up. The final rounds started at noon today. Catching up is not going to be easy.

Suddenly, my highlights are interrupted by a text message from Dad.

How's your mother?

> Okay, I guess. She's eating.

Try to cheer her up.

> Sure thing.

Tell her to call me when you're settled in the hotel.

> Sure thing.

Thanks, son. And go Jags! Picks are looking good. This could be the year!

> Yeah. Go Jags.

Mom's finishing her salad, and I'm desperately scanning the diner for something cheerful to talk about. My eyes land on a big plastic container on the counter by the register. From behind its translucent walls, four of Fanny's blueberry muffins are calling to me. They give me an idea.

"Hey, Mom, since we want to hit the road early tomorrow, how 'bout we buy those blueberry muffins. That way we won't have to stop for breakfast in the morning."

She looks at me with startled pride. "That's a great idea, Sam."

Our waiter emerges from the kitchen just in time. Re-energized, Mom asks him to pack up the muffins and add them to our check. We leave the Four Square Diner and make the short drive back to the Mountaineer Inn one last time. If I play my cards right, I can catch most of the draft coverage. If I feel like it.

"I'll get the first shower," I tell her, "and you should call Dad."

"Great idea, Sam." And just like that, our focus shifts to the journey home.

The sun is barely up, but the Jeep is loaded, the hotel key is turned in, and Ashe County is in the rear-view mirror. Mom's sipping on instant coffee from a paper cup and I'm chugging a vending machine orange juice.

"I'm looking forward to getting home," she says. "We'll get our laundry going first thing. While it's washing, I'll get my head together for this week's classes, and you can make sure you're ready for school. Dad said he'll grill some steaks. I'll make a salad. A home-cooked meal. It'll be great." She takes a deep, cleansing breath and lets it out slowly.

Ever since talking to Dad, she seems to be in a state of acceptance, even though nothing seems right. Bob Parsons has that effect on people. Mr. Practical.

"Ready for a muffin?" I ask.

"Sounds great." She tries to smile, and I try too.

I spread napkins on the console and break open the muffin box. They may not be fresh out of the oven, but these things are delicious. "Whoa! Great blueberry muffins," I say.

"They are certainly quite good. I wonder if Fanny would share the recipe. Maybe we could write to her in care of the diner..." Her voice trails off. She bites her bottom lip. "Or maybe we can just experiment. We can try out different recipes."

"Hey, summer's coming," I offer. "It can be our summer project." Mom is big on summer projects.

"Sure," she says. And this time she smiles for real. Like she's truly happy to be looking forward. Maybe the rear-view mirror is exactly where Ashe County needs to be.

I finish my muffins and instinctively pull out my phone, but then I remember. Still no data. I've really got to ration it better next month. I scan the Jeep for a distraction. I pick up a pile of homework from the floor, knowing there are still a few things I need to do. But there, beneath my homework, is *The Haunted Mesa* – the book I snagged from Uncle Buster's shelf before the entire library disappeared.

I slink down in my seat and get comfortable. "I think I'll delve into the world of Louis L'Amour. See what the Western genre has to offer."

Mom chuckles. "You do that. Let me know what you think." Nothing pleases an English professor more than seeing a young person read. She finds some classical music on the radio and we each recede into our own worlds.

The story opens with this guy named Mike Raglan who's alone in the desert at night. He's supposed to meet somebody who hasn't shown up. I'm caught off guard by the fact that he's traveling by car, and that he saw a Navajo family in a pick-up at one point. This is not the old Wild West shootout I thought it would be. Instead, it's a little on the creepy side, so I'm hooked. I love a good scare.

I turn the page with anxious fingers and it makes a crackling sound. The pages are kind of yellow and dry, and the glue is disintegrating along the paperback's spine. I sit up and try to flatten the pages open on my lap, hoping to reshape the book into a readable form. Unfortunately, the front cover is stiff and resistant.

I hinge the stubborn cover back and forth a few times like a door. Then my eyes catch something that's written on it, neatly, beginning at the top left-hand corner. *This book belongs to Buster Munroe.*

My mind jumps back to the Last Will and Testament of Buster Munroe and my heart pounds like a bass drum. The signature. This isn't big, round, middle-school-girl cursive. No, these letters are long, thin, and slanting sharply to the right.

Mom sways her head slowly with the rhythm of a cello reverberating through the empty space in the car. She seems to be in a state of forced relaxation, and there's no way I can upset her right now.

But there's also no way I can possibly believe that the signature on that will actually belonged to Buster Munroe.

# Fifteen

Dad splashes hot sauce on his over-easy eggs and guzzles coffee from a Jaguars mug. To look at him, you'd think the big guy might be a morning person. But he's not.

I'm slumped over the kitchen table trying to bring myself back to reality. Mom hums while she stirs her coffee, singularly satisfied with her idea of getting up early for a big breakfast on a Monday. I hope this doesn't become a regular thing.

"A new week. A fresh start." She's working hard on this attitude shift.

"Coach Kelly is going to cover practice today," Dad says. "I'll be home early to give you two a 'Welcome Back' celebration. I'm thinking a little *Aloha* chicken, some of my famous coconut rice, and a Monday night movie. One of the good old black and whites."

Dad loves old movies. Detective stories, mysteries, comedies, Humphrey Bogart, Cary Grant, you name it. If it was made in black and white, he'll eat it up.

"Well..." Mom reverts to her cautious face. "Let's see how much homework Sam has first. He's already missed a few days of school, and—"

"Sam, buddy," Dad cuts her off and pats my shoulder. "Try to get it all done before supper."

"We'll see," Mom says. And the conversation is closed.

I finish breakfast, clear my plate, and head to my room, where I send a quick text to Oscar. I never totally caught up on the draft or on his *War and Peace* text thread.

> Hey, I'm back! Meet you at the auditorium doors?

It's where we meet every morning, so it really goes without saying. But I figure I should reconnect. Especially because I still have 67 unread messages from him. I wait a few seconds for Oscar's reliably automatic response. But it doesn't come.

I go ahead and brush my teeth and gather my things, and just before sliding the phone into my backpack, I check one more time. Still no response. Weird.

The whole way to school, Mom is a free-flowing fountain of reminders, for herself and for me. "Remember to take that note to the office. Ask every teacher about make-up work. Oh, I need to post a reminder about final exams. Did you remember your lunch?"

It's kind of a relief once I'm out of the Jeep and back in my old surroundings. So much has happened, but everything here has stayed the same. Kids pour out of cars and gather in huddles of laughter and secrecy. Teachers are on auto-repeat shouting, "*WALK! NO RUNNING!*" and "*PUT THOSE PHONES AWAY!*" Berries are being plucked from bushes and thrown at human targets, and desperate procrastinators are hurriedly trying to finish meaningless homework assignments. Ah...the sweet familiarity of normal middle-school chaos.

I walk through the mayhem, around to the side of the school, and wait by the bus loop in front of the auditorium doors. Oscar's bus must be running late. I check my phone one more time. Still no response. I start to text again, but I'm busted.

"Put that phone away, Mr. Parsons!" Mrs. Alvarez is standing guard at the corner. I slide the phone into my backpack, and the bell rings. *Here we go.*

My first three classes are uneventful. Teachers are beginning reviews for final exams and I'm trying to stay awake. When lunchtime finally arrives, I head for the picnic table just outside the cafeteria doors. I always bring my lunch, but Oscar usually buys.

Halfway through lunch, I have the sneaking suspicion that either Oscar has been vaporized by aliens, or he's avoiding me. My food is gone and I'm curious, so I start walking. I put a hand up to shade my eyes and peek through the cafeteria windows. He's definitely not in there.

Next, I cut through the breezeway to the courtyard where students are scattered across the ground. Still no Oscar. There's really no other area to eat, so I'm baffled. And then I hear laughter coming from behind me. Several voices are involved, but the high-pitched, wheezy chuckles are distinctively Oscar's.

I turn to see Oscar and Joey Sabatini, along with three stuck-up members of the lacrosse team, stretched out on the concrete just inside the school entrance. Two huge, empty pizza boxes fill the space between them.

Joey's the first one to spot me. "Parsons!" he yells. "You're alive!"

"Yeah, I'm alive," is my clever comeback. *You're an idiot, Sam.*

"You're too late for pizza. We devoured it."

While Joey and his entourage exchange high fives, Oscar stands up, brushes his jeans with his hands, and walks closer to me. "What happened to you? You just quit responding to my texts."

"What happened to *you*?" I know I sound defensive, but does he really expect to play the victim here? "I tried texting you last night and this morning."

"Oh. Yeah. I don't have my phone this week."

"Don't have it? What happened?"

"My mom grounded it. She caught me texting with Joey after midnight Saturday night. I told her it wasn't a school night, and then she told me I didn't make the rules around here, and I said it's not fair, and she said life's not fair.... It was a whole thing." Oscar stares at the ground like he's studying the puddle of words that just spilled out and landed on the concrete. He finally looks back up at me and says, "At least you got my message about lunch. Where were you this morning?"

"This morning?" I suddenly realize I may have missed a few items of importance buried somewhere in the 67 messages I never read. Gotta think fast and recover. "Oh, yeah, how did that go?"

"It was all right, I guess. The field house was a little far from first period, so I was almost late. But I made it. Wanna go there tomorrow?"

"To the field house?"

"Yeah, duh. To the field house to hang with Joey and the lacrosse rats before school. Did you leave part of your brain in the mountains?"

"Yes! No! Sorry – I guess I'm a little distracted by everything that's happened." Oscar tilts his head and squints. I want to tell him about the funeral and Mountain-Aire Homes and the will and the signature. But I can't figure out where to begin, and then the bell rings.

Joey runs up behind Oscar, taps him on the back of the head, and says, "See ya, Hot Dog."

"Hot Dog?"

"Yeah, get it? It's my nickname for Oscar Meyer." Joey wraps an arm around Oscar and squeezes a little too tight. "Later, Parsons." Then he turns and yells, "Wait up!" He runs to join the lacrosse rats, leaving the empty pizza boxes behind on the concrete.

Oscar picks them up and carries them to the trash can. We walk to Spanish together, and he says, "I'm not sure I like that guy."

"Give him a chance," I say. "He's just in a totally different league from us."

"Yeah, I guess. So how was the funeral?" Oscar asks.

"Weird. I have so much to tell you. I don't know where to start." I decide to dive in and talk fast. "There's this company called Mountain-Aire Homes that's buying up land, and there's a will that leaves all of Uncle Buster's property to my mom's aunts, but the signature is definitely not legit. One of the aunts sells real estate, and she's working with Mountain-Aire Homes to try to turn all the property into a tourist trap."

"Why do you care? You didn't even want to go." Oscar has a point, but *ouch*.

"I know, I know. But I went. And now I know that something fishy is going on." As we enter Spanish class, I hang close to Oscar and follow him to his desk. "Oscar, I'm pretty sure that Uncle Buster was–"

"*¡Silencio, Señor Parsons!*" Mrs. Patsovas puts one arm between Oscar and me, and she points the other one across the room toward my desk. "*Siéntete, por favor.*"

After a mind-numbingly silent class period spent on written translations, I walk with Oscar to the only other class we share. Of course, it's pre-algebra, and there will be no opportunity for discussion. On the way there, I try to fill him in on more details, but Oscar's mind is in a different place.

"Hey Sam," he says, "as soon as you get a chance, I need that twenty bucks. I'm afraid my mom might start asking questions about where all my allowance went."

"Sure thing. Tomorrow." And I'm wondering if he's heard a word I've said.

100

There's no opportunity to talk in pre-algebra. The entire period is filled with test review. The exam will cover 45 questions in 50 minutes. Oh, the irony.

Finally, it's the last period of this grueling day – life science – and my solitary aim is to look like someone who's paying attention. My mind keeps scrolling through the events of the past week. It's like an involuntary process.

At dinner last night, Dad was talking about the importance of cutting your losses and knowing when to move on. Keep the good memories. Some things are just out of our control. Mom nodded right along with him. *How could she do that?!* Three times I almost brought up the signature, but I didn't. However, I'm keeping *The Haunted Mesa* in a very safe place, just in case it comes in handy.

"Sam?" Mr. Ogawa yanks my brain back into the classroom. He's standing at the white board, marker in hand, apparently waiting for an answer from me. My face grows hot as I realize all eyes are on me and I have no idea what the answer is. To be more precise, I have no idea what the *question* is.

The bell rings and Mr. Ogawa asks me to wait. Which means there's no way I'll see Oscar before he gets on his bus. But I wait.

Everyone exits and Mr. Ogawa moves closer. Sits in the desk next to me. "Sam," he sighs. "I know there was a recent death in the family. If you need to talk about it, I'm here, your guidance counselor is available..."

"No, I'm fine," I tell him. "I'm sorry. I just have a lot on my mind."

"I understand." He takes a deep breath and returns to his usual business-like tone. "While you were out, we enjoyed a guest lecturer from our local chapter of the Audubon Society. We discovered fascinating details about various bird species, and we discussed threatened and vulnerable birds. It was really quite astounding."

"Sounds like it." I nod, raise my eyebrows, try to look interested. Truly, this sounds neither fascinating nor astounding.

"It was!" he affirms with genuine enthusiasm. Poor guy. Must not have much of a life. "Now, for the month of May, we're scheduled to work on individual projects."

*Of course. It's May. Individual project time. Slide toward summer.*

"So, for this project, you'll need to select one of the priority bird species from the National Audubon website. There are quite a few birds on the list. Read a little about each of them and find one that truly ignites your passion. Be prepared to name your bird tomorrow. If you have any questions, feel free to email me. Once you get into that website you can really become absorbed. It has—"

"Got it, Mr. Ogawa. Thanks. May I go now?" I try to look pitiful. Play on his sympathy.

"Oh, well, yes. That's all, Sam." He sighs. "Remember. Priority birds. Let me know at the beginning of class tomorrow."

"Got it." And with that, I'm out the door. *A bird that ignites my passion? This guy really needs to get a life.*

I see the Jeep waiting in front of the school and sprint toward it.

"No worries, Sam. You don't have to rush. I figured you might be getting directions for some make-up work." Mom's obsessed with what I may have missed at school.

"Yeah, Mr. Ogawa was explaining a project to me."

"You missed a project?" Her volume and pitch are rising.

"No, no. Just the directions. I have to choose a bird to study. I'll pick it tonight."

"I'll tell your father the movie is NOT a good idea." She's been waiting to say that.

"Mom, really, it's no big deal. I'll have everything done by dinner." I'm trying to make a mental list of my homework, but thoughts of Bertie and Bess and Uncle Buster keep crowding my psychic space. I hear Carl's voice in my head, and I see June sitting silently, shadows beneath her sad eyes. I have to say something. I have to let it out.

"Mom, do you really think it's fair that Aunt Bess and Aunt Bertie can just take everything Uncle Buster loved and destroy it?" There, it's out.

She fakes a shocked look. "Sam, it's rightfully theirs. Uncle Buster left it to them. They can do what they want with it. It's no longer our business. Let's not talk about it."

Her words are dripping with Dad's practicality. But *he* wasn't there. *She* was. She knows something isn't right. We avoid conversation the rest of the way home.

My afternoon is filled with math homework, vocabulary review, and an informative article about the rights and responsibilities of United States citizens, complete with comprehension questions. I finally finish when I hear Dad's voice from the kitchen.

"*Aloha*, family! I picked up some pineapple and shredded coconut. Supper will be ready in an hour. Prepare your appetites!"

I walk into the kitchen and Dad locks me in a bear hug. "Life is good, son!" Either he really missed us, or he's really glad to have an afternoon away from spring practice. Maybe it's both.

Mom emerges from her office. She's been glued to her laptop ever since we got home. "Bob, thank you for cooking dinner. I'm slammed reading essays. Take a few days off and the work piles up."

"I hope you'll be ready for a Monday night movie." Dad's eyebrows are raised in hopeful expectation. He's really serious about this movie thing.

"I'm trying," Mom sighs. "What about you, Sam? Homework finished?"

"Check. Completed it all," I respond triumphantly.

"Which bird did you select for your project?" she asks. *Ugh. The one thing I forgot.*

"Oh, I'm narrowing it down. This Audubon site is fascinating." I pivot quickly so they don't see the eye roll.

Back on the laptop. Audubon.org. Priority birds. "Audubon's priority bird species are birds of significant conservation need, for which our actions, over time, can lead to measurable improvements in status." *Yeah, this sounds fascinating all right.*

I'm tempted to settle for the first bird on the list, the American Oystercatcher, but I figure that seems too obvious. Let me scroll down a few rows so it looks like I really put some effort into it.

Arctic Tern...*maybe.* Bald Eagle...*too famous.* Bobolink...*can't say that with a straight face.* I jump down a few rows and something catches my eye. Little gray birds that look like somebody took bright yellow paint and swashed it across the tops of their heads and wings. Their eyes wear black masks, and the feathers beneath their long, sharp beaks form a black triangle. It's the little blackbeards from Uncle Buster's place.

Golden-winged warblers. Warbler. Where have I heard that name? I remember! It's the Wi-Fi password at the Four Square Diner. This is weird. Maybe it's a sign.

Golden-winged warblers. Scientific name, *Vermivora chrysoptera.* These birds are threatened? I can tell you where to find plenty of them. Mr. Ogawa, I have found my priority bird species.

105

# sixteen

"*Mmm, mmm, mmm.* Bob, thank you for cooking. It's so nice to be eating home-cooked meals again, right Sam?" Mom seems genuinely at ease. My mouth is full, so I nod. I guess the voices of the past week haven't been playing in her head all day. Maybe there's something wrong with me.

Dad swells like he's being literally inflated by the praise. "It's great to have this household back to normal," he says. I'm asking myself, *normal? Are things really normal?* And then he turns to me. "Sam, your first year of middle school is about to come to an end. How does that feel?"

My mind catapults back to August. A lifetime ago. The awkward days at the beginning of the school year, trying to find classes, forgetting my locker combination, figuring out where to meet up with Oscar. And look at me now! I just might have a chance to get in tight with Joey Sabatini. "It feels good," I hear myself say.

This conversation train is off and running. It routes us through the entire school year. We're talking, we're nodding, we're laughing. Before I realize what's happening, we're drowning in *normal*. We're a *normal* family eating a *normal* dinner in a *normal* house. The train just keeps moving. And suddenly, the Ashe County drama that has so consumed my mind seems somehow smaller, less significant, distant. Almost like a passing dream. A few more weeks and summer will be here.

It's like Dad can read my mind because he says, "We need to talk about summer vacation. You know, every year we've made a trip to North Carolina. But this year, we're wide open. I'll miss the old tradition, but hey, let's think of some new possibilities."

Mom jumps in and says, "Your father and I were already coming up with a list. We could drive up the east coast, maybe take in Washington DC, Boston, New York."

"Or we could stay close and hit the beach," Dad says. "Atlantic coast, Gulf coast... take your pick."

My mind is reeling, but this time it's with imagined possibilities for the future. Dad's right. It's wide open now. We're no longer tied to Ashe County. We're free to explore. So I toss out an idea. "How 'bout Canton, Ohio?"

Mom tilts her head and looks puzzled. But Dad immediately smiles. "Canton, Ohio. Home of the Pro Football Hall of Fame!" We high-five.

"Ohhhh," Mom rolls her eyes and grins. "I have a feeling I might be outvoted on this idea!" Then we all laugh again, and it feels clean and good and uncomplicated. I have to admit, Dad's *Aloha* chicken was a great idea. And maybe he's right about moving on.

Once we get the kitchen cleaned up, Dad dims the living room lights and forces us to get comfortable in our seats. It's time for the big reveal. Which black-and-white treasure has he selected? Honestly, I don't care. I'm comfortable in the overstuffed blue chair, where my elbow is propped carefully on the "Home Sweet Home" throw pillow that conceals my phone.

Just in case the movie gets boring and I want to do a little stealth surfing.

"*Arsenic and Old Lace*," Dad says. "It's a classic, starring the incomparable Cary Grant. Lots of laughs in this one. You're gonna love it."

Dad finishes his intro and sits down with the remote. He's genuinely excited. Mom and I exchange a glance, and I can tell we're thinking the same thing. We'll humor him. He's a good guy.

So *Arsenic and Old Lace* turns out to be this whacked-out movie about two spinster sisters who run a boarding house. They seem like a couple of sweet old ladies up front, but they're actually homicidal maniacs. Lonely old men rent rooms from them, and they poison the poor guys by putting arsenic in their drinks. They look at it as charity work!

Cary Grant shows up playing their nephew and goes spastic when he lifts the lid on a cedar chest and finds a dead body inside. He learns that his crazy cousin (seriously, the dude thinks he's Teddy Roosevelt) has buried additional bodies in the cellar. Teddy thinks he's digging the Panama Canal, and the sisters tell him these old guys succumbed to yellow fever. Dark humor for sure, but some crazy antics. Dad is cracking up.

Some strange criminal dudes straight out of Frankenstein show up and the movie starts to lose me. I stretch out and lean over the throw pillow, sliding my arm underneath. I position my head so it's still facing the TV, but I can easily cut my eyes to see my phone. Perfect cover. Let the surfing begin.

Social media. *Same ol', same ol'*. Jags. *Nothing new*. A lot of speculation about next year. Pro Football Hall of Fame. Looks awesome. *Brilliant idea on my part*. I think about texting Oscar, but then I remember. He's currently without a phone.

So I tune back into the movie. Arsenic. How can you let two old ladies poison you and not even realize it? You know, wouldn't these guys taste it? I decide to do a little research and see if this plot holds water. Hey, if I'm caught on my phone, I can tie it back to the movie.

The first article that pops up says arsenic is "virtually undetectable" and "fatal in small doses." *Creepy*. But okay, I guess the guys wouldn't taste it or see it. Symptoms "mimic common diseases such as food poisoning." *Gross*. Next article. Exposure to even small amounts of arsenic over a period of time can produce symptoms like abdominal pain, convulsions, vomiting, neurological effects, cardiovascular effects. Geez, seems like there would have definitely been a mess for the loony sisters to clean up.

And suddenly, I freeze. Why does this sound familiar? My hands are trembling, and my mouth goes dry. *Virtually undetectable. A mess to clean up. A chair to cover. Vomit. Convulsions. Cardiovascular effects. Looks like a heart attack.* What if it was arsenic that killed Uncle Buster? Not from June, not from Carl, but from the two loony sisters who had the most to gain from Uncle Buster's death?

My heart is racing and I can hardly breathe. The phone falls from my trembling hands and slips behind the cushion of the overstuffed blue chair. No, it couldn't be. They didn't even arrive until Monday night, after Sheriff Frank Waverly found him.

But then I remember the odd story. The one about Jud seeing Uncle Buster through the window on Sunday. Carl Leibowitz said that was impossible, and he was right. It made no sense. Why lie about such a thing? *Unless* you had something to cover up. *Unless*, to kick off your weekend rendezvous, you swung by on Friday and secretly slipped arsenic into your brother's Salisbury steak. *Unless* you needed everyone to believe he was still alive all weekend, just in case someone had seen your big pink Cadillac sedan.

Their words come back on an echoing loop in my head. *The doily, the vomit, the Salisbury steak, right over left, the pocket change. Three quarters and two nickels...* And suddenly, it's so obvious. Too many details. I smell a lie.

# Seventeen

It's been a week since the big movie night revelation. I haven't said anything to Mom yet, but I've got two research notebooks going. The first one, which stays out on my desk in plain sight, is filled with information about golden-winged warblers.

While I wouldn't say the little blackbeards have *ignited my passion*, I'll admit they're growing on me. They live in an early successional forest habitat. That basically means old fields and farms that are covered with tall grasses, young trees, and shrubs.

In other words, an early successional forest habitat is exactly what Uncle Buster had before Gruntin' Jud Waverly took the bush hog to it. Over the past 40 years, the number of golden-winged warblers has steadily declined, largely due to loss of habitat. Thanks, Jud.

There's actually an organization called the Golden-winged Warbler Working Group dedicated to these little birds. A bunch of biologists conduct research, and they work with other groups to restore early successional forest habitats. That's great. But fat chance they'll ever restore Uncle Buster's place. It's becoming a tourist habitat instead.

My second research notebook is hidden between my desk and the wall. It's where I'm collecting evidence that will prove, beyond the shadow of a doubt, that Uncle Buster was intentionally poisoned.

111

Once I've built an airtight case, I'll talk to Mom. When she's firmly on board, we can present the evidence to Dad.

The first thing I need to do is establish a motive. Aunt Bertie seemed pretty clueless, so I'm devoting my efforts to the infamous Bess Munroe. And for her, it all boils down to one motive: MONEY. I have plenty of evidence to support this fact:

- ✔ *Her real estate business is not doing well.* I checked out *buyfrombess.com* and discovered there are no recent listings. Every property she represents has been stagnant for a while.
- ✔ *Her Smith Mountain Lake House is for sale.* That's right. The vacation cottage she bragged about has been on the market for six months. And the price has been reduced twice already.
- ✔ *Uncle Buster's property will bring in fast cash.* The Mountain-Aire Homes group wants to get their project up and running. They figure the resistant neighbors will fall like dominoes once Uncle Buster's acreage is developed. Mountain-Aire Homes is prepared to pay for that property, and Aunt Bess is ready to deliver.

*So, ladies and gentlemen of the jury, I have established a clear motive for Bess Munroe, and that motive is spelled M-O-N-E-Y.*

But what about accessibility? How could she have placed arsenic in the food eaten by our victim, Mr. Buster Munroe? She lives in another state. And at the time the arsenic was placed in

112

his food, she was tucked away in her Smith Mountain Lake cottage. She has a watertight alibi.

*Or does she?* Are there any witnesses who actually *saw* Aunt Bess at her Smith Mountain Lake cottage? Perhaps the real story is that she made a trip to Ashe County that Friday and slipped some arsenic into Uncle Buster's Salisbury steak. And just in case someone spotted ol' *BYE-BESS* in town, the obvious lie about Jud seeing Uncle Buster alive and well through his front window on Sunday afternoon was a cover.

But, you might ask, what leads me to the conclusion that arsenic was the weapon of choice? Well, according to my research, a large dose of arsenic causes multisystem organ failure, which leads to death. And the signs and symptoms of arsenic poisoning closely parallel the victim's experience. They can also be mistaken for signs of a heart attack:

- ✔ *Red or swollen skin.* It would be hard to tell with all that make-up the funeral home put on him, but a red face and swollen skin could easily be passed over as signs of heart disease.
- ✔ *Abnormal heart rhythm.* Also consistent with a heart condition.
- ✔ *Lesions in the skin.* Perhaps the open wounds on Uncle Buster's hands were actually the result of arsenic poisoning rather than a fall or a skirmish.

✔ *Tingling of fingers and toes.* That could easily explain why he fell down. The loss of sensation in his feet caused him to lose his balance.

✔ *Nausea and vomiting.* Check. The aunts clearly stated that they cleaned up vomit at the scene.

Suddenly, I realize Mom is standing in my doorway and I jump. "I didn't mean to startle you, Sam. Wow, looks like you are really bogged down with work."

"Yeah," I chuckle, maybe a little too nervously. "Just trying to work on this bird research."

"Well, I felt bogged down, too. End of semester papers are coming in, and I'm tweaking my final exam. I decided to take a break and go for a walk. Care to join me?"

"Uhhh..." I'm stalling while I try to decide if this is a good time to tell her about my *Arsenic and Aunt Bess* theory. Probably not. I need to have the evidence thoroughly laid out when I present it. "No, I'm good," I say. "I think I'll try to power through and finish." I still need to find the missing link that ties Aunt Bess to Uncle Buster's poisoning.

Mom shrugs and smiles. "Well, don't work too hard." And she's off.

Back to my laptop. I have an important question to answer. Where would a person go about finding arsenic? In the old days, apparently you just walked into a drug store and asked for some rat poison. Thankfully, it's not that easy to acquire anymore.

Today, most arsenic is used in things like paints, dyes, and pesticides. It also occurs naturally in rocks and soil. People can be exposed to arsenic through drinking water when pollutants run off into water systems or when wells become contaminated.

This is scary stuff. But it doesn't explain how someone could personally acquire some arsenic. Hmm. If I could just figure out where she got it, I could possibly find a way to trace the purchase back to her. Receipts, surveillance cameras, records from an online transaction...the missing link.

Suddenly, my phone buzzes and breaks my concentration. Seems like Oscar got his phone back.

Sam.

Glad to see you're back in the 21st Century. What's up?

NM. Going 2 Jumping Jax w/ my church group in 2 days. Need my $20.

Jumping Jax is a trampoline park that just opened, and I've been dying to check it out. I wonder momentarily if Oscar might invite me along. But I think he's waiting for a response.

Sorry I keep forgetting. I'll get the money right now and put it in my wallet.

Thx. Meet in the old spot tmw?

We've been meeting Joey's squad out by the field house every morning, which is technically not a school-sanctioned place to hang because there's no supervision. However, since I don't actually have any classes with Joey, my bro-bonding time is very limited. I'm not sure how to handle this.

> What's wrong with the field house?

IDK. Feels weird.

> I'm getting close. Just one more week, okay?

Suddenly, I hear the front door slam. That was a short walk. Mom's forceful footsteps pound through the living room and into the kitchen. She sighs loudly and slams the kitchen counter. Sounds like she needs attention.

> Okay, I gotta go. See you tomorrow at the field house.

CU tmw.

I find Mom leaning against the kitchen island taking deep breaths. In slowly...hold for four seconds...out slowly. It's something she learned in yoga class. While she tries to coax her body into relaxation mode, her right hand clenches a letter. She's already half-crushed one side of it.

"Is everything okay?" I ask. Stupid question, but it's all I can come up with.

"It will be," she exhales. "I'm sorry, Sam. Everything's fine." In for four counts...hold...and, "It's just something I had put out of my mind, and..."

Her voice trails off, and she's back to a four-second inhale. I move a few steps closer and try to read the mail that seems to have set her off. Along one edge I can tell it's a bill for $500. I lean forward and the rest comes into focus. It's from the Law Office of Hicks and Honeycutt. Payment for services rendered. Due upon receipt.

# Eighteen

It's Thursday morning, and I'm speed-walking to the field house. Trying to hurry while still looking basically casual. I'm running late because I had to go back into the house. I finally remembered Oscar's $20.

Only one more day and our Joey hangs will be reduced to lunch. But I have an idea. Dad's team will be playing in the Duval County Spring Jamboree next week. Oscar and I always go, and I thought we could casually extend an invite to Joey. Since he likes football and all.

I arrive with a good five minutes before the first bell and the place is desolate. A little morning mist hangs in the air, but no Joey. No lacrosse rats. No Oscar. Very weird. I check my phone. No message. I wait until the bell rings, and then begin a brisk walk through damp grass.

Suddenly, I hear my name echoing from the hall. It's Assistant Principal Morales. "Follow me, Sam Parsons," she says as soon as she sees me turn towards her. "I'll let your first period teacher know you'll be late." I trail behind the *clop, clop, clop* of her heels on concrete with no indication of what this is about.

We head straight into her office, where Oscar sits staring at the floor. Assistant Principal Morales motions to a second chair and says, "Sit." I obey. "Sam," she continues, "our school resource officer was making her rounds this morning and found

Oscar out by the field house. This is an area with no supervision, and it's off limits to students before school."

I cut my eyes toward Oscar. He's still focused on the carpet. Morales' eyes are on me. "We are quite certain some other students were out there as well, but Oscar has been unwilling to divulge names. He says he doesn't know of anyone else. He says you had arranged to meet him there to return something to him."

I swallow hard and suddenly feel like I've entered an alternate universe. The only two reasons I've set foot in the office have been to pick up my class schedule and to deliver an attendance note. I've certainly never been in trouble. Same for Oscar.

"Um, I borrowed $20 from Oscar. I was going to pay him back this morning." I dig the crumbled bill out of my pocket as evidence. Finally, Oscar looks up. He seems annoyed.

Morales isn't finished. "And why is it you chose the field house to settle this debt?"

I swallow hard, not sure how to respond. "I thought it would be discreet."

"Yes," she counters, "and this is what concerns me. Only people with something to hide take chances trying to be discreet. I am quite certain there is more to this story."

"It was my idea," I tell her. "Oscar didn't want to meet there." Finally he looks up. Maybe there's forgiveness in his eyes?

But Morales doesn't skip a beat. "I will be calling your parents about this matter, and I will let them know you'll serve detention this afternoon. Meet me in room 508 after the last bell. That will be all."

"Yes, ma'am," we say in unison. We're handed hall passes and escorted from the office.

Before we part ways, Oscar stops and says, "Can we *please* go back to meeting at the auditorium doors?"

"Yeah," I tell him. "It's okay, because I have another idea for how we can hang with Joey. Listen to this–" I want to tell him about the Spring Jamboree plan I've come up with, but he won't listen.

"Please," he interrupts me. "Can you just give me the $20 already?"

I realize the money is still wadded up in my fist. "Yeah," I say, a little annoyed at being shut down before I could reveal my great idea. "Sorry I kept forgetting. It's only twenty bucks. I don't get why this is such a big deal."

Oscar unfolds the bill and looks at Andrew Jackson. "Easy for you to say, dude. I couldn't pay for Jumping Jax yesterday, and I had to come clean about the whole thing. My mom was pretty upset. Wait 'til she hears about detention."

We stand there for a minute, and I think he has something more to say, but apparently not. He finally turns and walks away.

I'm kind of stunned and confused all morning, and I can't tell if it's my imagination, or if people are actually whispering behind my back. Seriously? It's not like I *murdered* somebody.

At lunch, I wait for Oscar to buy his food, and then we meet Joey and the rest of his foursome at the usual spot. "Parsons and Hot Dog!" he yells. I can't read his expression. "I hear you got caught at the field house. Shame on you." His entourage laughs. "We cleared out as soon as we heard the buzz of the R.O.'s golf cart. Oscar stayed. He was waiting for you. Sucks for him."

More laughter. But not from Oscar. He's staring at Joey and not looking at all friendly. "We got a detention," Oscar tells him.

"Welcome to the club," Joey says. "Morales gave me a detention for excessive tardies. Now I'll be late to lacrosse. Ironic." He nods to his squad, visibly impressed by his unusual show of logic and vocabulary.

We sit down on the warm concrete and Joey continues to crack jokes about the whole detention thing. He doesn't seem bothered by it at all. He says, "Morales thinks she's all that. Watch me shift the power dynamic."

The rats laugh, and Oscar looks like he might be ill. The sun is in his eyes, so he squints at Joey. "Did they call your parents?"

Joey leans back, his lanky arms outstretched behind him. "Good luck," he says. "They're on a trip to New York for my dad's work. The school called my sitter. She's cool. She's in college."

121

Oscar's obviously upset, but I'm starting to see this as an opportunity. I can tell Joey about the Spring Jamboree after school when his friends aren't around. That way I won't get accidentally roped into inviting the lacrosse rats.

On the way to Spanish, I want to tell Oscar about my Spring Jamboree idea, but he's not in a very good mood. Finally, I have to ask. "What's up with you?"

"Are you kidding me?" I wait for what follows, but he seems to think the totality of his mood has been implied in that one question.

"Are you upset about the detention? We *never* get in trouble. This is one time. It'll blow over."

Oscar stops in his tracks. "One time?" he says. "Have you noticed that since we've been hanging with Joey bad things keep happening?"

"No," I tell him, "what are you talking about?"

Oscar shakes his head and starts walking again. His back is to me, but I hear him loud and clear. "For somebody so smart, there sure are a lot of things you don't notice."

After the last bell, I go straight to room 508. Oscar's already there, but he doesn't acknowledge me. Assistant Principal Morales paces back and forth with growing irritation. Joey finally struts in and sticks his hand out toward me for a fist bump, but Morales steps in front of him. "That will be enough,

Mr. Sabatini. This isn't social hour." She's obviously rattled. *Power dynamic. I get it.*

Morales continues. "For thirty minutes, you will sit. No talking. No reading. Nothing. You will sit and think about your actions." She looks at her watch like she's synchronizing a military maneuver. "Time begins now."

Over the course of thirty minutes, Joey takes a nap, Oscar stares out the window, and I mentally rehearse my arsenic indictment like I'm preparing for a courtroom drama.

When time's up, the three of us exit as one unit and stroll casually along the corridor. Joey stretches and says, "Great power nap. Should help my lacrosse game."

"Hey, speaking of game..." not my best segue, but I don't have much time; it's a short corridor. "My Dad's got this high school football thing coming up next Friday night. Should be fun. Want to go with us?"

"What kind of football thing?" Joey looks interested. Oscar looks like he just got punched in the gut. Not my fault he wouldn't listen to my idea this morning.

"It's a Spring Jamboree. Teams from all over the district take turns playing. Their bands and cheerleaders come. There's food. I mean, it's not the Jaguars, but it's a pretty good time."

Joey stops walking and smiles. "You and Hot Dog think this thing is fun?" My sales job must be pretty good. He's interested.

"Yeah, it's a lot of fun. Right, Oscar?"

"Yeah," Oscar says. "I guess so."

"Sure thing. Text me the deets!" And with that, he high fives his goodbyes and heads for a small car driven by a scowling young woman. Somebody's not in a good mood.

Right behind her, Mom stands on the running board of the Jeep and yells, "Oscar, I told your mom I'd give you a ride!" Her voice sounds calm, friendly even.

I'm sensing a vibe that says Mom finds this whole detention situation kind of petty. So I climb in the front seat and say, "I don't know what the deal was with Mrs. Morales today. Weird, right?"

"Oh, I'll tell you what's weird. Getting a phone call that my son, who I trust to be responsible, has a detention for being in an unauthorized area. And as if that's not enough, I get a second call from Oscar's mom letting me know you owe him $20 for some football bet."

So I guess I misread the vibe.

"I'm sorry," I say. "I gave Oscar his money, and we won't be going to the field house anymore."

Oscar is silent in the back seat. Finally, Mom says, "We'll discuss this at home."

The tension remains thick all afternoon, and before dinner, the inquisition begins. "What were you thinking going out to an unsupervised area?"

"We've only done that a few days," I tell them, stretching the truth without actually lying, "just trying to get to know this kid Joey. He doesn't have a lot of friends." *A play on Mom's heartstrings. And next, a hook for Dad.* "I think his father works with the Jaguars organization somehow."

But Dad's a step ahead of me. "So the whole reason you lied about Mrs. Alvarez, the math test, the 88.9%... is because you wanted to watch the draft and put up money against a kid with connections?"

Dad looks satisfied with his logic. Mom looks like someone just pulled the floor out from under her. "I just can't believe you would lie..." she says, shaking her head.

"Mom, I'm sorry. I didn't realize it would be such a big deal."

Dad's ready with a practical precept. "Anytime you have to lie, it's a big deal."

Then Mom swoops in with the emotional hit. "And in case you didn't notice, that $20 was a *big deal* to Oscar. You put him in a very awkward position."

They're both silent for a minute, letting that sink in. I picture Oscar at Jumping Jax, unable to pay his admission. And then having to come clean to his mom. Yeah, I guess awkward is an understatement. And I guess it was actually my fault.

"I'll apologize to Oscar," I finally say. "And I was thinking that maybe we could start fresh and invite Joey to the Jamboree with us next week."

Silence again. A couple of deep breaths. Finally, Mom says, "Maybe. Give me contact information for Joey's parents, and I'll think about it."

"And give me your phone," Dad says. "I'll be taking possession of it until next Friday."

I go back to my room to retrieve my phone, but before handing it over, I hurriedly send two messages. I text an apology to Oscar and the Jamboree deets to Joey.

# Nineteen

After a not-so-good-night's sleep, I stumble toward the kitchen but stop in the hallway. There's a hushed conversation in progress.

"Five hundred dollars is a lot of money," Mom whispers. "I had no idea. I just thought–"

"We can manage." Dad cuts her off. Speaks softly. "Don't worry about this."

"But it was just a consultation."

"On a Saturday."

"He didn't even do anything."

"He's a lawyer."

"It was thirty minutes."

"Time is money."

"We're trying to plan a vacation–"

"Eva, please. It will all work out."

Loud sigh. And then silence. I take that as my cue to enter, and I figure it's a good time to apologize. Somewhere in my tossing and turning I realized I never did that. I start with, "Good morning."

Mom turns away, but Dad says, "Hey, son."

The mood seems to have moved beyond my whole detention scandal, but I don't let that derail me. "I just want to say I'm sorry. Really."

Mom turns toward me now, and I see that she's been crying. She lunges forward and hugs me.

"Just one more thing before we classify this as water under the bridge," Dad interjects. "If $20 is of so little consequence to you, I think you should find someplace to donate that amount. Think about it and get back to me."

Sounds reasonable. I nod. Mom lets go. Pats me on the shoulder and smiles through her puffy eyes. Then we eat breakfast and talk about the weather.

Once I'm at school, I head straight for the auditorium doors. Perfect timing. Oscar is stepping off his bus and things are beginning to feel almost normal.

"Did you get my text?" I ask.

"I don't know. I'm currently without a phone. Again."

"Oh," I say, "I just wanted to tell you I'm sorry."

No response.

"Are we good?"

Oscar shrugs. "I don't know."

"If it makes you feel any better, I don't have a phone till next Friday."

He looks down, stifling a laugh. This is encouraging, so I continue.

"I also have to find someplace to donate $20."

He looks up now. "Yeah, I had to hand your sorry-looking Andrew Jackson over to my mom to repay the youth director. And then I had to write a letter of apology to go with it. And for the next month, my allowance will go straight into my college fund. What a night."

"Forgive me?" I ask, and offer a fist bump.

Oscar reciprocates the fist bump, sort of smirks, and says, "Yeah, I guess."

The first bell is still ten minutes away, so I say, "Hey, you won't believe the latest developments in my murder investigation."

"So now it's a murder investigation?" He looks skeptical. "I thought this whole thing was about your aunts and some millionaire development company."

"My mom's aunts," I correct him, "and it's called Mountain-Aire Homes."

"I thought the dude had a heart attack."

"Get this – the symptoms of a heart attack can be very similar to the symptoms of arsenic poisoning." I relay the solid motives I've compiled for Aunt Bess, the sketchy story about Gruntin' Jud seeing Buster through the window, and end with the signature on the will.

"Wow," Oscar is understandably shocked. "Sounds like you *could* have a murder on your hands." I smile, finally able to spill the details to someone who understands. "Or, it *could* be that your aunts realized their brother's health was failing and reacted by securing the property with a will. You know, a lot of people don't have wills. The state decides who gets their property. It causes problems. It's a whole thing."

"You don't believe me?"

"It's not about whether I believe you or not. If you're going to be able to prove anything, you need a paper trail."

"There's a will with a phony signature."

"Dude, that's a breadcrumb, not a trail."

*A paper trail. That's what I need.* And with that, the first bell rings.

The long-awaited Friday finally arrives. Oscar and I both have our phones back, and Mom has arranged to pick Joey up at his house. I get to see the swanky place for myself, and the three of us can do a little bonding away from the lacrosse rats.

We pick Oscar up first and he climbs into the back seat wearing his St. Johns River High School t-shirt, just like Mom and me. I hope Joey doesn't think that's lame. We're kind of all dressed alike.

The GPS routes us to a gated community along the river. Mom talks to the guard stationed at a brick security booth and then sails through the entry as the wrought iron gate retracts. Pretty soon, the GPS lady announces, "You have reached your destination," and Mom pulls into a circular drive in front of a massive stucco house with gargantuan columns flanking the front door.

I pull out my phone. "I'll text Joey and let him know we're here."

"Absolutely not," Mom says. "The appropriate thing is for me to meet his parents. I've only had a phone conversation with Joey's mom."

The three of us exit the Jeep and walk up the granite steps to ring the doorbell. Through the door's glass panes, we see the scowling young woman moving toward us. She opens the door and asks, "Can I help you?"

"I'm Eva Parsons." Mom sticks out her right hand but the sitter looks at her with confusion. "I'm here to pick Joey up for the Jamboree."

The sitter immediately puts off a *this is awkward* vibe. "Joey's not here," she says.

"That's odd," Mom says. "I arranged this with Mrs. Sabatini days ago."

"Well, the Sabatinis are in New York right now, and Joey just left with one of his lacrosse buddies to go to Jumping Jax. It's a new trampoline park. Sounds cool."

Oscar mumbles, "Yeah, I've heard of it."

"Well, thanks," Mom says. "I guess we got our wires crossed."

I decide to move to the back seat with Oscar, and as we climb into the Jeep, he says, "Can we just go back to eating lunch at our old spot?"

I get it, and I'm feeling conflicted, but then I think of the Jags. And club seats. I feel like we're so close. "Just one more day," I hear myself say. "We need to at least hear his side of the story."

131

# Twenty

I can't sleep. It's Sunday night, the eve of my last week of sixth grade, and my brain is stuck in this continuous loop. It begins with my warbler presentation. Which is tomorrow. And it counts for my final exam grade. And let's say I've been a little distracted.

Next stop on this runaway mental train is the whole Joey thing. I only have a week left before summer break, and I thought the Jamboree was going to make us solid. Did he think the Jamboree was stupid? Or did he just forget? Do I bring it up at lunch tomorrow or just let it slide? Oscar wants to give up on the whole Joey thing. He's still sore about the detention. And the money. *That twenty bucks was a big deal to Oscar.*

Twenty bucks. What about five hundred dollars? That sends my brain to Byron Hicks. And arsenic. And my lack of a paper trail. I have no doubt that Aunt Bess poisoned Uncle Buster with arsenic, and I've got a notebook full of rock-solid proof. At least it looks rock-solid to me. But what if I'm going crazy? After all, some kind of conspiracy-theory gene might run in the family.

I haven't sprung the theory on Mom yet. She's hard to pin down. When she mailed the $500 check to the Law Office of Hicks and Honeycutt, Mom vowed to adhere to the "out of sight, out of mind" principle. I'm afraid if I bring it up now, I'll send her spiraling back into worry. But I can't just keep this to myself.

Once I reach that point in the loop, it's a full-speed, downhill run through the whole cast of characters: Aunt Bertie, Aunt Bess, Jud, Carl, June, Kyle, Fanny...a blur of faces and places and words and birds. Little golden-winged warblers.

That brings the train back to school, where final exams are looming like vultures circling above me, and I have a presentation to make. Tomorrow. And here we go again.

I must have fallen asleep eventually, because the blaring alarm propels me out of bed, and before I know it, I'm sitting at the kitchen table staring into a bowl of soggy wheat flakes, freeze-dried berries, and little rocks of granola. Mom is buzzing around the kitchen inventing new project ideas. Her community college semester is over and she's looking for ways to stay busy.

Dad stands at the counter with a map spread out in front of him, a pencil behind his ear, and a yellow highlighter in his hand. Old school. I don't know what the guy has against modern technology.

Mom buzzes up to him. "What do you think about painting the laundry room?"

Dad smirks playfully. "Isn't it already painted?"

"Oh, really, Bob," she tries to seem annoyed, but she can't help smiling.

Dad's making vacation plans for the second week of June. He's plotting our course to Canton, Ohio. "Practically a straight shot up I-95 to I-77," he says.

Mom stops, and I look up from my cereal, suddenly and soberly awake. Straight up I-95 to I-77. That's pretty much the way we traveled to Uncle Buster's place every summer.

Dad senses the tension, and there's an awkward silence.

"You know, we don't have to rush getting up to Canton, Ohio." Back to the map and highlighter. "If we slide to the west, we can go through Knoxville and Lexington. Maybe check out a couple of college campuses." He's reaching. The playful tone has been obliterated.

"Whatever you think, Bob." Mom straightens a magnet on the fridge, opens and closes a couple of drawers, and sighs. "Right now I need to focus on getting a few things done around here before we drive all the way to Timbuktu to see some football memorabilia." Definite tension.

Dad shrugs. "Well, no rush." He folds the map. "I better get to school. There are students anxiously awaiting my final exam. Grab your things, Sam. I'll drop you off so your mom can focus on her projects."

Mom opens her mouth like she's going to protest, but then stops. "Sorry, guys," she says. "I'm looking forward to vacation. Really."

A few hugs and we're off, warbler project in tow.

I don't plan to carry this poster and report around all day, so as soon as I get to school I go in the science building and stop by Mr. Ogawa's class to drop it off. He's at his desk, spectacled eyes glued to his laptop.

"Excuse me, Mr. Ogawa?"

"Uh-huh?" he responds, never looking away from his screen.

"Is it okay if I just leave my bird report here?"

He stops. Turns. Looks at me like he's confused, and then says, "Oh, Sam, yes. No problem." Then he's back to his screen.

On my way out of the classroom, I'm nearly trampled by Joey Sabatini and the lacrosse rats. They pause, swallowing laughter, and Joey says, "Hey, Parsons."

I didn't think I'd see him till lunch, so I'm a little unprepared. "Hey, Joey," I say. And then I decide to go for it. "We missed you Friday night."

He stops. Looks confused. "Friday night?" I guess he really did forget. "Oh yeah, my parents made me go to a thing."

"Oh," I hear myself say. Part of me wants to just leave it at that, but for some reason I don't. I can't. "That's weird. Because my mom had talked to your mom about the Jamboree, and it was all arranged."

Joey steps closer, but the rats back away and move toward the exit, still snickering at the hilarity of their own existence. "Yeah, so it was my dad," Joey says. "He wanted me to represent him at a Jaguars thing."

"At Jumping Jax?" I can't believe I'm not letting go of this thing. *Who am I?*

"Yeah, it was kind of last minute. The Jags were throwing a party for needy kids. It was a charity thing. Needy kids and all."

"That's cool," I hear myself say. Even though I know he's lying.

135

"Later, Parsons," And I just stand there as Joey Sabatini turns and walks away. He disappears through the door of the science building, letting it slam with a deafening thud.

I'm about to text Oscar and tell him we'll just meet at our old lunch spot when the bell rings, the hall fills, and my last Monday of sixth grade officially begins.

My first two classes slog by slowly with mind-numbing exam review. Third period is looking the same when suddenly an announcement interrupts the monotony. *Please send Sam Parsons to the front office.* Confused, I stand and walk, partly thankful for a break and partly nervous. The last time I went to the office, it didn't work out so well.

An eighth-grade assistant at the reception desk gives me a condescending sneer and says, "Just sit down. I'll let Mrs. Morales know you're here."

Moments later, I see Oscar being escorted from Morales' office by a guidance counselor. His face is beet red, and I can't tell if he's angry or if he's been crying. Maybe it's both.

The eighth grader returns and says, "She'll see you now."

Mrs. Morales stands at her office door, eyes narrowed, mouth frowning.

"Mr. Parsons, we meet again."

"Yes, ma'am." I enter on trembling legs and stand frozen in confusion.

"Sit," she commands, motioning toward the chair I sat in just a few weeks ago.

She closes the door. "Tell me what you know about the graffiti found in the boys' restroom."

"Which restroom?"

"This is no time for games."

"No, really. I mean, I haven't seen any graffiti."

"Mr. Ogawa tells me you were in the science building before the first bell today. Is that correct?"

"Yes, I was leaving my bird report in his classroom."

"And did you use the restroom while you were there?"

"No, ma'am."

"I see." She takes a deep breath. "So I suppose you didn't write on the bathroom walls."

"No, ma'am." *Does she really think I would do that?*

"Well, someone left a derogatory message and made it appear as if it were written by Oscar Ruiz."

"Oscar wouldn't do that."

"Oscar also would not divulge who *might* have done it. Seems like he's trying to protect someone." She narrows her eyes like she's using some invisible force to penetrate my brain.

"What did it say?"

"You tell me."

"I honestly don't know."

"Let's take a little walk, shall we?"

I follow Mrs. Morales to the science building. The boys' restroom is dramatically marked with an orange cone and an "Out of Order" sign. She holds the door open and watches closely as I read the words scrawled on the wall in thick black marker:

## MORALES IS A SCUMBAG.

## SIGNED, OSCAR

## AKA HOT DOG

My hands involuntarily clench into fists and my chest tightens. The game's up. Club seats were probably never in my future anyway, and even if they were, this is too high a price to pay. "Mrs. Morales, I know exactly who did this."

After I explain everything in detail, basically sealing my fate as the school's biggest snitch, Morales sends me back to class. And I thought I couldn't concentrate before. Now my mind reels in a hundred directions and my hands won't stop shaking.

Finally, lunch time arrives and I go to our old spot, fully expecting Oscar to be there. But he's not. I've got to find him and truly apologize for this whole Joey thing. So I walk. He's not in the cafeteria and not in the courtyard. Instead, I find him in the least likely place – standing on the concrete at the school entrance, face to face with Joey Sabatini.

"...not *funny*!" I hear Oscar say. I missed what came before, but I'm sure I can fill in the blanks.

"It was plenty funny," Joey responds. "Morales *is* a scumbag, and you're a loser, Hot Dog. You follow your little dweeb friend around like a puppy."

"This has nothing to do with Sam."

"Aw, that's so cute, Hot Dog. Now you're gonna stand up for Parsons. Talk about a loser. Wanna go to a *Jamboree*?" Joey drags that last word out in a painfully mocking tone, and the lacrosse rats double over laughing. But Joey doesn't have time to laugh because Oscar suddenly throws a right hook to his jawbone.

I'm momentarily paralyzed in a bubble of shock and disbelief. Somehow, Oscar's voice – loud, sharp, and resolute – penetrates the bubble and I hear the words: "Don't call my friend a loser, and DON'T CALL ME HOT DOG!"

With that, Joey lunges at Oscar and they're locked in a grabbing, jabbing huddle. The rats all back away, but I can't do that. I run toward them, determined to peel Oscar away from Joey Sabatini.

Suddenly, Mrs. Morales appears. Her stern tone is able to break up the wrestling match and a few minutes later, I'm sitting in her office. Again. But this time, Joey and Oscar are there, too.

*Disappointed. Outraged. Calling your parents. Detention.* These words lay on my shoulders like weights. This is all my fault. Oscar and I are given detentions and released to go back to class. Joey, on the other hand, has to stay in the office. First, he has to clean the bathroom wall. Then he's on in-school suspension for the rest of the week.

As we stumble toward Spanish side by side, I look at Oscar's face. His eye is bruised and his lip is cut, but somehow, he seems more okay than ever before. "I'm really sorry about all

139

this," I say, wondering how long it will take him to forgive me. "Another detention. Because of me."

"No," he says. "*This* detention is because of me." And then my best friend smiles, busted lip and all, and says, "Sometimes, you just have to take a stand."

# Twenty-One

It's nearly impossible to study. Of course, it's not my phone that's distracting me, because once again, it's been grounded. No, it's the paint fumes that permeate every inch of breathing space and the '90s boy band music that's blaring from the living room speakers. I gather my books and decide to study on the patio.

Mom's in the kitchen scrubbing paint from her hands. "I know it's not Friday yet, but I'm thinking pizza for dinner. I have a lot of clean-up to do."

I stop. Nod. "Sure."

"Where are you headed? Don't you have some finals to study for?"

I hold up the stack of books as an answer.

"Oh, Sam, was my music bothering you?"

"Maybe a little. And the paint smell is making me kind of woozy." Her face drops. Guilt. I need to smooth it over. "It's okay. It's nice outside."

"Sam, I'm so sorry. You go study. I'll air out the house." As I open the sliding glass door, she flips on the hood fan over the stove and silences The Backstreet Boys.

Outside, it's not much better. The air is warm and still, and mockingbirds screech at each other from the short, tangled trees and thick bushes. But it's not just that. I *need* to concentrate. I purposely left the secret notebook safely hidden behind my desk. Eliminate temptation. Just a few finals to get through and then school's out. I can do this.

Pre-algebra exam tomorrow. Focus, Sam. Nothing you can really study here. Just review the notes and quizzes. Rework any problems you missed. Get your head in the zone. There's one right answer. Find it.

The sun is sinking as I move on to World Geo terms. I flash through them quickly. That final is two days away. After that, English. And then I'm free. No finals in electives, and Mr. Ogawa's bird report counts as the final exam for life science. The end is in sight.

I stack up the books and lean back in the wrought iron chair. The mockingbirds have quieted down and the air is cooling. A gentle breeze blows across the patio. I close my eyes.

And like an unwelcome intruder, Oscar's words enter my head. *You need a paper trail.* The only solid documentation I have is a signature in a book. Anybody who compared the signatures on the will and in *The Haunted Mesa* would know that Buster Munroe did not sign that will.

Also, I have my own notes about the effects of arsenic. The symptoms correlate with those Uncle Buster experienced, but if there's one thing I've learned in science, a correlation doesn't prove anything. I need to prove that arsenic was the *cause* of death. But there wasn't an autopsy.

Then I remember something said by Barney Baldwin, the funeral director. And repeated by the lawyer, Byron Hicks. *The state takes a vial of blood to analyze.* If I'm right, they should find arsenic in his blood. Who do you call to find out about that analysis?

The slamming of the front door interrupts my thoughts, and I hear Dad's voice yell, "Dinner's ready!" Through the sliding glass door, I see him set a large pizza box down on the kitchen counter and turn off the hood fan. He closes the front windows and sorts through the mail before disappearing into the bedroom.

While he lets Mom know the pizza's here, I stack up my books and take them to my room. The house, now absent of the blaring '90s pop, is filled with an eerie silence. By the time I make it back to the kitchen, Mom is noticeably absent, and Dad is leaning over the counter staring at a piece of paper. I squeeze in next to him and read:

> *Dear Eva,*
>
> *I thought you might like to know that June's father passed away over the weekend. That Kyle fellow came up to her house, and I sat in on the meeting so she wouldn't be alone. He had all the legal paperwork prepared locally by the Law Office of Hicks and Honeycutt. June's got 30 days to find another place to live. I thought you might want to send a sympathy card while you still knew where to reach her. I'm sure that would mean a lot to June.*
>
> *Yours truly,*
> *Carl*

Dad turns the envelope back and forth in his hand like he's looking for something. He shakes his head. "Your mother's a little upset. She said we could eat without her."

"It's not fair, Dad." I can't hold back. "Mountain-Aire Homes is leaving June without a place to live. It's not right." We pull two stools up to the kitchen island and eat our pizza over paper towels.

Dad chews, swallows, thinks. "Well, I'm sure June's father negotiated a fair sum for the property, and she can use that money to begin her new life."

His words sound hollow and his face is grim. No attempted diversion about school business or summer vacation. This is affecting him.

"Dad, Mr. Leibowitz owns the property next to June and across the road from Uncle Buster's place. He'll be sandwiched in by vacation cabins. How long do you think he'll last?"

Dad takes a deep breath and sets what's left of his pizza slice down on the paper towel. "I don't know, son. Things change. Carl will have to come to terms with that."

Again, his eyes are dark and sad. His voice cracks. I can't help myself. I see an opening.

"I know you don't want to discuss this, but I need for you to hear me out. It's about Uncle Buster."

Another deep breath. He sits up straight, looks right at me. His face offers more of an invitation than a protest. So I continue.

"The will. We saw it—"

"I know," he interrupts.

"But Dad, there's something you don't know. Something Mom doesn't even know."

He rests his elbow on the island, leans his weary head against his fist. I go on.

"The signature on the will stood out to me. It had big round letters. I thought it was kind of an unusual way for a guy Uncle Buster's age to write, but I didn't think much more of it—" I hop off the stool. "Until..."

I run to my room and grab the book. While I'm at it, I wrestle my investigation notebook out from behind my desk. Just in case this conversation goes well.

Hopping back on the stool, I turn to Uncle Buster's signature and push the book toward Dad. "This signature – it's not the same. Not even close."

Dad studies the long, leaning script. Then he shakes his head, rubs his eyes. "But this doesn't prove anything, Sam."

Now is as good a time as any. I push the paper towel and pizza aside and put my notebook on the island. "There's more."

For the next hour, Dad listens patiently while I go through my research. Arsenic poisoning, the symptoms, the oddly disguised chair. I tell him about Aunt Bess delivering Mountain-Aire Homes flyers and the curious involvement of the Waverlys. I lower my voice when I describe the apparent coziness between Aunt Bess and Jud.

Finally, I tell him the obviously fabricated story of Jud seeing Uncle Buster through the front window on Sunday evening. I end with Uncle Buster's death sequence as described by the aunts, complete with the doily, the vomit, the Salisbury steak, right over left, and 85 cents – *three quarters and two nickels.*

Dad doesn't speak, but his silence says volumes. He's not dismissing my theories, not trying to argue. I end with a nod to his logic. "You know how it goes, Dad. Too many details. I smelled a lie."

The hint of a smile bends the corners of his mouth. "Well, something doesn't add up, but we can't jump to conclusions just yet."

*Yet.* That's a promising word. I want to ask him more, but we're interrupted by the ringing phone. *Seriously, who uses a landline anymore?* I'm not expecting him to answer it, but he does.

"Hello?" He pauses, listens for a moment. And then he says, "No, she can't come to the phone right now. Why don't you just relay the message to me, Bertie."

He scrambles through the junk drawer and pulls out a pen and notepad.

"Uh-huh." He writes something down. "Okay, well that's generous. We'll talk and get back to you." More scribbling. "Yes, I understand... Yes, I wrote it down... Okay, now. Goodbye."

I'm waiting to hear what that was all about, but Dad doesn't even acknowledge me. He makes a beeline for the bedroom. Usually, he tries to get Mom's mind off this stuff. But not now.

146

My appetite returns, so I scarf down a few pieces of pizza while I wait for news. Finally, after about 30 minutes, Dad emerges from the bedroom, cell phone in hand.

"Sam, we're taking a little unexpected trip," he says. "I've booked a room for us Sunday night. At the Mountaineer Inn."

# Twenty-Two

The rest of the week flies by. Somehow, it's easier to let go of the Uncle Buster saga and concentrate on finals when I know that *something* is happening. Even though I don't know what that *something* is.

Apparently, Bertie's phone call was an offer. She and Bess talked it over, and they decided Mom should really be the one to own Uncle Buster's place. They're ready to sell it to her for a fair price.

Mom plays emotional ping-pong. One minute she's hopeful, the next minute she's angry. Then she's racked with guilt on her way back around to being happy about this strange offer.

Dad spends most of Saturday at the high school wrapping up grades and packing up his classroom. Mom and I spend the day packing our bags and creating a multitude of theories. It's both exhausting and invigorating.

*Guilt. They can't live with the guilt. Or maybe someone discovered the fake signature on the will. Busted. Jud couldn't take it anymore. He came clean on the whole thing. Or maybe it's the vial of blood. It came back with some incriminating evidence....*

We stop our conspiracy theory game when Dad gets home. Happy to have him in on the situation, we know not to push it too far. We eat a smorgasbord of leftovers to clean out the fridge and load the car for an easy getaway. And for this trip, I make sure to pack my laptop and investigation notebook.

Sunday's drive is leisurely and surprisingly upbeat. We don't discuss anything about Bertie or Bess or Uncle Buster. Mom and Dad sing along to their *Best of the '90s* CD collection while I move beyond the signature and actually finish *The Haunted Mesa*. Pretty cool sci-fi western. And somehow, it makes me feel a little closer to Uncle Buster.

Along the way, we stop in small towns and eat at local restaurants. Dad's in no particular hurry, and Mom enjoys strolling through quaint little sidewalk boutiques. "Keeping the mood light," Dad tells me.

Finally, just as the sun is beginning its descent behind the Blue Ridge Mountains, we pull into the parking lot of the Mountaineer Inn. Dad checks in while we wait in the Jeep. He emerges with the room key, dangling from the familiar green plastic rectangle, and we enter our "deluxe" room, also known as a room with two double beds and a little wooden table.

Mom gets the AC window unit cranking while Dad and I unload the car. Soon, we're sitting in the TV-less silence discussing this strange turn of events.

"My guess is that something fell through with the Mountain-Aire business," Dad says.

Mom scrunches her face. "But that doesn't completely make sense. Mountain-Aire Homes is moving forward with their claim on June's property."

"True." Dad rubs his whisker-stubbled chin. "So just why do your aunts seem so desperate to sell? Bertie was trying to hide it, but I'm telling you, she was desperate."

I remind them that I've done a little research on Bess, and that her financial situation seems, well, desperate.

Mom nods. "Hmm...." The wheels are turning. But then they come to a grinding halt. She frowns. "But it doesn't make sense. They stand to make more money from the Mountain-Aire deal than they would from us."

Dad sighs. "No point in making wild guesses. We're meeting them up at the house tomorrow at 9:00. Should we venture out early and find a local place to get a good, old-fashioned mountain breakfast?"

Mom and I immediately lock eyes and smile. She says, "Yeah, we know just the place."

So, of course, we find ourselves entering the Four Square Diner bright and early for our Monday morning breakfast. Of all people, Kyle the skinny-tie guy is standing at the counter talking to Fanny.

"I'm telling you," Kyle says. "You could make a fortune! Picture it." He swings his hand from left to right like he's underlining an imaginary billboard. "Fanny's Country Muffins." Fanny waves her hand and dismisses him, but I see a hint of satisfaction on her face.

Suddenly, Fanny looks beyond Kyle and sees us. "Well, look what the cat dragged in!" She comes out from behind the counter with three menus in hand. First, she hugs Mom and me, and then she introduces herself to Dad.

"Welcome, welcome." She leads us to our booth. "I know what these two like to eat for breakfast, but what about you, Big Fella?"

Dad scans the menu and orders a Western Omelet with hash browns and a side of country sausage. Mom tilts her head and pretzels her eyebrows disapprovingly, but she doesn't say anything. She's always trying to get him to go for the healthier choices.

Just before Fanny walks away, Dad says, "Oh, and can I also get one of those blueberry muffins? I've heard a lot about them."

Fanny smiles. "Sure thing, Sugar."

When she delivers our food, Mom asks Fanny about June. "I was hoping she might be here this morning."

"Oh, honey," Fanny says, shaking her head, "she's busy packing up that old house. Carl Leibowitz is lettin' her store stuff in his shed. Lots to keep. Lots to get rid of. It's just so sad."

Mom frowns. "Has she found a place to live?"

"She's still lookin'. Might have to stay at the Mountaineer Inn for a bit if she can't decide on somethin' soon."

"Well, if you see her, please let her know we're in town. I don't want to bother her, but I sure would love to give her a hug."

By the time Mom finishes her conversation, Dad is halfway through his greasy feast, and I've nearly obliterated my pancakes. "Well, it looks like you guys were hungry!" Mom gently blows on a steaming spoonful of oatmeal. "Mmm," she says, "just as good as I remembered."

While we're waiting for her to finish, Dad and I split the giant blueberry muffin. Breakfast dessert. That should be a thing.

"Wow, you weren't kidding!" Dad pulls back and looks at the muffin. "This is delicious."

I glance over at the counter. Fanny tries to maintain her tough exterior, but she can't hide a satisfied smile.

After settling up at the diner, we make the trek up to Uncle Buster's place. Or I guess I should say Bess and Bertie's place. The winding road that leads toward the mountain seems frozen in time. Wood-frame farmhouses stand in front of tall barns and long chicken coops, all surrounded by rows of vegetation. The plants are taller, I guess, but other than that, nothing has changed since Mom and I were here.

As the road begins to climb, farmland fades into forest. Brick homes are tucked between trees and surrounded by bushes. Behind them, the forest rises tall and thick as it ascends the foothills. We're getting close. I notice Dad easing up on the accelerator.

As we pass June's driveway, Mom cranes her neck, but there are no signs of life. We slow down at Carl's mailbox, but the front of his property is so thick with growth you can't see his house from the road.

Dad makes the sharp turn onto Uncle Buster's driveway, and Mom and I gasp simultaneously. It's practically lifeless. The house sits alone atop its hill. Trees, bushes, barn...they've all vanished. Across the desolate, empty field, a large bulldozer sits poised against the forest. No doubt, those trees will be the next to fall.

# Twenty-Three

Before the dust settles around our Jeep, Bertie is on the front porch. Her right hand waves limply while her left hand presses a tissue to her nose. She wears a long yellow robe or kimono — I'm not sure what to call it.

"Here we go," Dad says. We open and close our doors in unison, then walk single file along the narrow strip of concrete that leads to the porch. No trees, no bushes, no birds. It's eerily quiet.

"Let's hurry inside and close the door," Bertie gripes from behind her tissue. "I guess we need rain somethin' terrible, because this dust is just awful!"

*Hello. Ever hear of erosion?* I think it, but I don't say it. *Could it be you've cleared away every plant whose roots held the soil down?*

As soon as we're all inside, Bertie slams the door behind us and removes the tissue from her face. "Sam, I think you've grown more since we've seen you! Eva, what are you feeding that boy?" Bertie tries to cut through the tension with idle conversation, but every jaw remains tight. Mom's arms are crossed and Dad's hands are in his pockets.

"Wellllllll..." An exaggerated Southern drawl and a cloud of flowery fragrance precede Aunt Bess, and suddenly, there she is, gaping as if surprised by our visit. She's wearing black yoga pants and an oversized "Buy from Bess" t-shirt. Her nails are painted a deep red, and her dark hair is pulled back in a ponytail. *The casual murderess look.*

Bess plunges right into hugging everyone, forcing Mom's body language to shift into a more vulnerable position and Dad's hands to leave the safety of his pockets. His arms flail a little, trying to decide whether to return the hug. *Definitely awkward.* But just like that, the casual murderess captures the power dynamic.

She starts asking questions about the weather in Florida, our summer plans, and Dad's predictions for Appalachian State football this fall.

While small talk is exchanged, I sneak some sly glances around the scene of the crime. I make a mental list of several changes, knowing I'll need to wait until we're back at the Mountaineer Inn before I can record them in my notebook.

The old throw rug has been replaced by a large, rectangular area rug. One end is curled up a little, like it hasn't been unrolled long enough to settle. Uncle Buster's favorite chair – the one that was mysteriously covered last time we were here – is gone. In its place there's a glider-rocker that's made of fake logs with painted-on "wood" grain. There's a matching couch along one wall, lined with red plaid cushions reminiscent of Paul Bunyan's flannel shirts. A throw pillow on one end of the couch says, "Cabin livin'." And of course, every cushion is topped by a crocheted doily.

Mom and Dad loosen up a little. Mom mentions our plans to visit the Pro Football Hall of Fame, and the aunts immediately counter with advice on alternate vacation ideas. This conversation gives me a chance to slide back and get a good look at the kitchen.

The Blue Ridge Building Supply calendar still holds its position on the wall, a lone survivor of a major wall-stripping. But all the photographs are gone, and where Uncle Buster's landline used to hang, there's an empty phone jack surrounded by a ghostly rectangle of unfaded paint.

The adults seem engrossed in conversation, so I slide my phone out of my back pocket. I hold it tight to my chest and open the camera app. I figure photographic evidence might come in handy. I can study the scene more closely once we're back at the inn. Kitchen wall. *Snap.*

The countertops are practically bare as well, except for a brand new single-cup coffee maker, a rotating carousel of coffee pods, and a gallon jug of spring water. Countertops. *Snap.*

It's the same table, but the entire surface is covered with cases of individual water bottles and several more gallon jugs. *Somebody's going a little overboard on hydration.* Bess's oversized black handbag rests in a kitchen chair. I guess it serves as both purse and briefcase for Madame Real Estate Agent, judging by the manila folders bulging from the top. Table and chairs. *Snap.*

"Sam, how rude of us. We have totally ignored you!" Bess walks over and grabs my right elbow, pulling me away from the kitchen and into the conversation. With my left hand, I slide the phone into my back pocket.

Bertie squeezes my shoulders. "I bet you got all As in school this year, just like my Arnie always did."

"How *is* Arnie?" Mom asks. "Has he found a job yet?" *I do believe Mom is trying to rattle Bertie's cage. And it seems to be working. A little shift in the power dynamic.*

Bertie's arms drop to her sides. She stiffens and sighs, "No, the right job just hasn't come along. Arnie is so smart, and such a great preacher. I think that's intimidating to a lot of churches. He just needs—"

"But we're not here to talk about Arnie, now are we?" Bess interrupts. "Let's all sit down and talk about this old house." She makes herself comfortable in the fake-log chair while Mom, Dad, and I line up along the flannel sofa. Bertie pulls a rocking chair over and completes the circle.

Bess begins. "We love this old place, but we just don't have the time to deal with it. Especially me. The real estate business is running me ragged!" she lies. She flashes a fake, toothy smile and drums her red-tipped fingers on the arm of her chair.

"Besides that," Bertie continues, "we know this was your home, Eva. We think Buster would've wanted you to have it." I still can't decide if she was in on the murder, or if she's just plain clueless.

I look at Mom and wait for a response. I sense the emotional ping-pong going on beneath the surface, so I'm glad Dad decides to speak. "I don't know much about this Mountain-Aire Homes group, but they seem to be pretty aggressive about buying land around here. We understood you were selling the property to them." *Good job, Dad. Cut to the chase.*

Bess leans back and takes a deep breath. "That is certainly an option we considered. It would be very lucrative." She tilts her head toward Mom and stretches her closed lips into an awkward grin. "But some things are more important than money."

That one catches me off guard. I nearly choke swallowing my incredulous laughter and dissolve into a coughing fit. Mom's attention turns immediately away from Bess. She pats my back and looks concerned. As I pull it together, Bertie says, "Eva has so many memories at this old place. It would break our hearts to let it slip out of the family."

Mom sits up straight, hands on her knees, and looks from aunt to aunt. "Well, you've already done so much redecorating. I would think *you'd* like to be the ones to keep it in the family."

Of course, Bess is ready with a response. "Oh, I come by these pieces of furniture easily in my business." A sudden idea improves her posture. "And we can certainly work them into the price if you'd like to keep them." *Always looking for an opportunity to make a buck.*

Bertie appears to be somewhere between excited and anxious. "Just think of it, Bob. You'd have your own mountain place to come and enjoy the great outdoors. Are you a fisherman?"

Bess doesn't even give Dad a chance to answer. She jumps up and heads for the kitchen. "Let me give you an idea of what we're thinking." She rifles a manila folder from her black bag and drops it in Mom's lap on her way back to her fake-log chair.

Mom opens the folder, gives it a quick scan, and closes it. "We'll have to discuss this, of course. We'll head back into town to read over your offer, and then get back to you." She tries to sound resolute, but I notice the folder trembling in her hands.

Bess raises her eyebrows and looks genuinely stunned. "Well, don't take too long," she playfully warns. "We might just get comfortable here and change our minds!" Both aunts erupt in laughter, and Mom seems to shrink.

Dad takes the reins. "We're all a little tired from traveling." He pats Mom's hand gently, and the three of us stand.

The hugging commences again and I feel like I need a shower. As Bess escorts us to the front door, I glance back in the hallway. There's something new there. Something I hadn't noticed on the way in. A large wooden chest stands against the wall.

"Hey Dad," I say, feeling rather bold. "This wooden chest remind you of anything?"

He looks confused. "Not in particular. Looks like an antique cedar chest."

Then I say it. I'm speaking to Dad, but I look directly at Bess. "Doesn't it remind you of the old chest under the window in that movie you love. You know, *Arsenic and Old Lace*?" I put emphasis on the word *arsenic*.

Dad chuckles and says, "Yeah, I guess it does, son." But it's not *his* reaction that captures me. At the mention of the word arsenic, Aunt Bess immediately drops her smile, and her face turns white.

"Huh. I guess I haven't seen that one," she mutters.

And just like that, the power dynamic is back in our court.

# Twenty-Four

The Jeep is in reverse, and Dad's arm is braced against the back of the passenger seat. But he's not looking out the rear window. He's looking directly at me. "Sam, what did I tell you about jumping to conclusions?"

"I was just making an observation." I look out the window, trying to break his death stare.

Finally, the car rolls backwards. An instant dust cloud forms, and Dad groans, "We're going to need a serious car wash after this."

Mom's eyes are fixed on the emptiness that used to be covered by thick rows of blueberry bushes and bordered by crabapple trees. Dad backs the Jeep alongside the garage so we can pull forward down the driveway.

But he stops suddenly. And he backs it up a little more. "Hmm." No words are needed. The garage door is open, and we all see it. In place of Uncle Buster's little car, long pink *BYE-BESS* is safely nestled in the garage. The really strange thing is, there's barely enough room to open the car doors because one wall is lined with large plastic garbage bags. They're stuffed full and tied at the top.

Mom sighs. "I guess they need to haul the garbage to the solid waste management facility. Uncle Buster never wanted to pay to have it picked up." She shakes her head and stares across the emptiness again.

161

We rattle down the rocky driveway and stop at the mailbox. I turn back and take a picture. Lonely house, desolate wasteland. *Snap.*

Dad's about to turn when Mom shouts, "Bob, wait!" He slams on the brakes and she studies the driveway across the street. Maybe hoping to see Carl. Maybe June. Maybe wondering if we should pay an unannounced visit.

And then something almost magical happens. A golden-winged warbler flits down from a tree and lands on top of Carl's mailbox. The little blackbeard sings as if he can't even see the devastation taking place just across the road. *That's it, little guy. Keep up the positive attitude.*

"It's okay, Bob," Mom concedes. "Let's just get back to the inn." As we turn out onto the road, I slide toward the window to take one last picture. Golden-winged warbler on a mailbox. *Snap.*

For the entire ride back to the Mountaineer Inn, Mom and Dad review the contents of the folder. I'm dizzy listening to the same revolving questions frame their conversation. *Why are they wanting to sell for such a good price? What's the angle here? Do you think Mountain-Aire Homes is pulling out of the area?* But never once do they mention the murder. I laid out all the evidence for them. What more do they need?

Finally, Mom gets the ball rolling on a plan of action. "What we should do is have a real estate agent look over these papers. Someone we trust. What about Rita Kelly?"

Rita Kelly is married to Dad's assistant coach. Billboards and bus benches all over Jacksonville display this huge picture of Rita Kelly in a navy blue suit, holding a cell phone to her ear and smiling like she just made a huge sale. The slogan "Ring Rita" is plastered above her phone number. Everybody knows who Rita Kelly is.

Dad counters Mom's idea. "I'm sure Rita would be glad to help, but I was thinking we should have a lawyer look over it. Seems like enough real estate agents have been involved."

Mom wastes no time responding. "Oh, I don't know how much I trust the Law Office of Hicks and Honeycutt! And they're the only lawyers in town."

"Tell you what," Dad proposes. "When we get back to the motel, I'll search up some legal options in close proximity. You ring Rita and run your questions by her."

Mom grins in agreement, and I'm feeling completely sidelined here. We should be contacting law enforcement. We can't let the aunts get away with this. Real estate agents, lawyers, contracts.... Bess has successfully created a diversion. My only hope is to continue going solo on this one. "If you guys go off on a lawyer hunt, can I just hang out at the inn? I'm pretty tired of being in the car."

They look at each other and shrug. Mom is the one to respond. "Sure, Sam. I know this can't be fun for you. We'll get an extra key from the front desk. You might want to go to the snack or soda machine while we're gone." And then she adds, "But try to make healthy choices."

163

I nod. "Sounds great." It sounds *perfect*, but I'm trying not to look too excited. After picking up a drive-thru lunch, we're back in the room eating from our separate bags and working on our separate agendas.

It doesn't take long for Dad to find a law firm. Smith, Williams, and Barnes is located in Alleghany County, at least a 40-minute drive from the inn. Mom has promised to scan a copy of the contract and email it to Rita's office from the Alleghany Public Library, where she has called to confirm there is indeed a scanner and computer she can use.

My first order of business is to upload the photos from my phone to my laptop. Then I'll add a few tidbits to the old investigation notebook, and perhaps I can figure out how to get the test results for that vial of blood they took from Uncle Buster.

"Sam, I hate leaving you alone when I don't know how long we'll be." *Uh-oh. Mom's having second thoughts.*

"It's a modern age, Mom. We can be in contact instantaneously. Call me. Text me. Send me an email. *If* you have internet access. I'll be here on the Wi-Fi." I smile a little sarcastically and she rolls her eyes.

"I know, I know," she says. "Call if you need us. Really." And finally, they're gone.

I fire up the laptop and connect my phone. I upload my five photos and do some editing to make them brighter, clearer. The bare yard and lonely house are kind of a punch to the gut, but the little blackbeard on Carl's mailbox makes me smile. Pretty nice image. Too bad I didn't have it for my report.

But let's focus on the evidence. The calendar, the rectangle where the phone used to be. Okay, no more landline, I guess. Doesn't seem that important, but I record it in the notebook.

Next photo. The practically empty countertops. I understand the appeal of upgrading the coffee maker, but it seems like a waste if they're not gonna be here long. And why the jug of water next to it? Are they too special to drink good ol' well water? I'm sure Uncle Buster would have something to say about that.

My only other shot is of the table and chairs. Of course, the table is barely visible under the cases of water bottles and extra gallon jugs. It looks like they're staging some kind of disaster relief mission.

The only other thing of interest is Bess's giant handbag. I zoom in on the manila folder protruding from the top. Probably another copy of the sales proposal. But then I notice a paper peeking out along the folder's edge. Only a splash of black ink is visible. I enlarge the picture and apply several filters, trying to discern any recognizable words.

And finally, I see it. Without a doubt, the first visible word fragment says -*eport*. Okay, it's a report. But the words jutting toward the margin just beneath that are the ones that cause my palms to sweat and my heart to nearly pound out of my chest. On that line, without a doubt, I see –*senic, ppb.*

I talk to myself out loud, desperate to share this with someone but completely alone. *A report that details arsenic parts per billion. What's measured that way? Liquid. That can only mean one thing. Bess got her hands on the analysis of Uncle Buster's blood sample, and I guarantee she doesn't want anyone else to see it.*

# Twenty-Five

*Okay, Sam. Be calm. Be rational. Think.* Talking to myself actually helps a little. I connect my laptop to the guest Wi-Fi, open a browser, and start searching. *State of North Carolina...death reports...coroner's office...medical examiner.* Bingo. North Carolina Office of the Chief Medical Examiner.

Autopsies, toxicology testing, document request. *Yes.* I click on the link. There's an online form to request toxicology results. *Is that what I'm looking for?* I'm guessing yes, but I'm required to supply a valid email address as well as a mailing address in case the results cannot be sent via email. *Okay, this could be tricky.* It would probably be best to talk Mom into filling this out, but right now she's on a different trail.

I search for contact information. *A phone number. That's it.* I'll make a call to Raleigh and see if I can get any info over the phone.

"North Carolina Office of the Chief Medical Examiner. How may I direct your call?"

I try to sound calm, serious, adult. "Yes, I'm calling to inquire about a toxicology report for a deceased relative."

"Okay, sir, let me put you through to our toxicology department."

*Sir. She's buying the act.*

The phone rings again, and a guy answers. "This is Brian in Toxicology."

*Calm, serious, adult...* "Hi Brian, this is Sam." *Should I have said my name? My heart is beating faster.* "I'm calling to inquire about some results of a recent toxicology, um, test." *Test. Is that the right word?*

"When was the autopsy performed?" Brian asks. *Is he suspicious?*

"There was not an autopsy, Brian, but it's my understanding that a vial of blood was collected from the deceased back at the end of April and sent to your office." *Okay, regaining my cool.*

"Gotcha. Well, the process takes a while, Sam, and those reports aren't ready for at least sixty days. We have an online form. You can submit a document request and we'll get the report to you as soon as it's available."

*How can Bess already have a copy? Is Brian lying to me?*

"I see. Um, it is my understanding that one family member has already received a copy of the report."

"No, not possible. It takes sixty days," Brian repeats. "But you can go ahead and fill out the document request form online. Is there anything else I can help you with?"

*I can't lose Brian yet.* "We in the family are just very concerned about the possibility of arsenic being the cause of death. We're eager to get some answers. Is there any way to expedite the process, Brian?"

"No, sixty days, Sam. But I can tell you right now that arsenic poisoning is pretty complex and can't be determined from a blood sample. We would need a tissue sample for that. Are you sure there wasn't an autopsy performed?"

My mouth goes dry. How can Brian be telling the truth? I have photographic evidence of a report that obviously contains a measure of arsenic parts per billion. My brain races in a million directions as I hear, "Is there anything else I can help you with?"

"No, no thanks," I manage to say.

"Okay then, have a good day, Sam."

"You too, Brian."

And that's it. A dead end.

I numbly make notes in my investigation notebook and then stare at the photo, trying to see anything beyond the obvious. There's no other explanation for *–senic ppb*. Could Brian be in on this? *Whoa, Sam. Now you're taking this whole psychic-conspiracy-theory thing to a new level. Take a break.*

I stand, stretch, put my phone in my back pocket, and pick up the room key. A little fresh air might be good right now.

I lock the door behind me and stroll to the snack machines. Healthy choices. *Hmm. That's a tough one, Mom.* I settle for balance. A candy bar and a bottle of water. Of course, once the water is in my hand, I think about the cases of water bottles and gallon jugs on Uncle Buster's kitchen table. Then the purse. Then the manila folder. Then I'm right back where I left off.

I can't go back to the room until I clear my head, so I decide to take a walk. The town's main drag is just down the hill and around the corner. I'll make a loop and see the sights. It's at least a couple of hours before the parents will be back, and I've had all the sitting I can handle.

At first, the early afternoon sun is in my eyes, blinding me, but once I turn the corner, it's more of a comforting warmth against my face and shoulder. I take a sip of water and look out at the mountain ridges that frame the town. Layers of gray-blue formations recede into the distance, and I wonder what it's like to wake up to this view every day. I kind of get why Uncle Buster never wanted to leave.

My back pocket buzzes once, and I jump. The phone. I need to empty my hands. Up at the next corner, I see side-by-side cans for garbage and recycling. I hurry to toss away the empty bottle and candy bar wrapper and pull out my phone.

> Waiting for Mom at library. Checked out official Jags site. Great piece on new defensive end. Have you seen it?

I want to say, *Are you kidding me, Dad? I'm a little busy trying to solve a murder!* But of course, I don't say that.

> Cool. Will check it out.

*That's a lie. Well, at least for now.*

> Sorry to leave you so long.

> I'm good. Take your time.

And I mean that. I need to make a game plan. However, for right now, I'm not going anywhere. Because I'm suddenly distracted by the most curious scene taking place right across the street from me. The notorious brothers, Gruntin' Jud and Sheriff Frank Waverly, exit the Four Square Diner together. Frank's face is grim, and Jud looks like... *maybe he was crying? What is this?*

They walk together toward Jud's big brown beast that's parked in front of the diner. The brothers hug, obvious emotion on each of their faces. Then Jud climbs into his truck while Frank turns and walks away.

Through the back window of Jud's crew cab, I see a large duffle propped up against his guitar case. *Going somewhere, Jud?* Then it occurs to me. Sheriff Frank was the first one at the scene of the murder. He was the one who sent the vial of blood to the Office of the Chief Medical Examiner. So wouldn't he be the first one to get the results?

Brian wasn't necessarily *lying* to me. He was following orders. Gag orders. The results are in, but they were released exclusively to law enforcement. They're being withheld from family members until the authorities gather enough information to build a rock-solid case.

So *what if* Frank was suspicious from the beginning? *What if* the toxicology results confirmed his suspicions? And *what if* he shared the results with Jud, who in turn shared them with Aunt Bess? Obviously, Frank is trying to protect his brother by getting him out of town before going public with the accusations against the aunts. It all makes sense. And perhaps the greatest revelation is that Frank Waverly can be trusted.

I turn and speed-walk toward the corner, quickly
formulating my plan. I'll go back to the inn and gather my
evidence. Then I'll present it to Frank. Suddenly, squealing tires
startle me, and a long pink car jumps the curb, narrowly
missing me. It continues across the intersection and whips into
the Weston Realty parking lot. Hugging a brick wall and trying
to calm my pounding heart, I watch *BYE-BESS* park crooked
across two spots.

A rush of adrenaline energizes me and diverts my course of
action. Time to be bold. Time to cross the street and face the
enemy. After all, *sometimes you just have to take a stand.*

Bess climbs out of her car and then reaches back in for the
black bag stuffed with manila folders. As she does, I sneak up
behind her on trembling but resolute legs.

"You nearly killed me," I say.

Bess, still leaning in and rifling through her bag, is startled.
She jumps and whacks her head on the way out of the car.

After a quick visual scan of the area, she straightens her
large form into a tall and imposing posture. "Well, what are you
doing wandering the streets all alone?" She fans herself with a
manila folder and blows tousled hair away from her pallid face.

"Just getting some air," I say. "And solving a little mystery."

Her eyes narrow and she leans toward me. "In other words,
sticking your nose where it doesn't belong?"

"You won't get away with this," I say, keeping a safe
distance and calculating an escape route.

"Just what do you think you're talking about?" she asks. For someone who was in such a hurry just minutes ago, she's suddenly very committed to this conversation.

"I know about the arsenic," I tell her. "I saw the report."

Her eyes widen and the folder waves wildly in her hand. "That's not possible!" she says too quickly. Then she takes a deep breath and attempts to backtrack. "What report? I don't know what you're talking about."

"Oh, you know," I hear myself say. "And you won't get away with this. Soon everyone will know it was *arsenic* that killed Uncle Buster. And they'll also know that *you–*"

"Miss Munroe! We're waiting!" My accusation is cut off by the sudden interruption of skinny-tie guy Kyle Jasper.

Bess turns and looks at him. "I'M COMING!" she barks. Then she turns back one more time, pointing at me with the corner of her manila folder. "I don't know what little game you're playing, but you'd better watch your step." With that, she turns, and after a few large strides, disappears into the Weston Realty Office.

And then I turn. And I run. Propelled by a conflicting mix of fear and impending satisfaction, I sprint back to the corner and plod up the incline toward the Mountaineer Inn as fast as I can. It's all coming together.

I get to our door and fumble with the key. It takes a few tries and several deep breaths before the lock finally relents. I grab my notebook first. *Do I write down the new clues or just present what I have?*

My pocket buzzes. Another text from Dad.

> At the law office now.
> Fancy waiting room.
> You still okay?

*Oh, I'm more than okay,* I want to tell him. *I'm about to bust this murder case wide open.* But I can't say that.

> Snacks and Wi-Fi. I'm good.

> Enjoy!

> Will do!

Actually, this helps. I can coordinate my time. They have to meet with the lawyer and then drive back. I estimate that gives me about an hour, or maybe a little more. *No time to write the new details, Sam. Just go with what you have.*

I gather my notebook and laptop, take a few deep breaths, lock the door behind me, and jog back down the hill toward town. I don't actually know where the sheriff's office is, but I figure it can't be far from the diner because Frank was on foot when he parted with Jud.

I'm walking now. I want to appear calm, cool, and collected when I approach Sheriff Frank. Once I pass the diner, I'm in unfamiliar territory. An antiques store, a clothing boutique, a pizza parlor. *Pizza? Mom, you were holding out on me.*

And just past the pizza parlor, I see the sheriff's office. Right there on the corner, gold star on a glass door. I grip my notebook and laptop tightly. *Am I ready for this? Can Frank Waverly really be trusted?* There's no time to lose. I'll have to go with my gut on this one. I pull open the glass door and a bell rings to announce my arrival.

A wooden counter runs the width of the building, and three doors are evenly spaced down the right side of the room. Frank Waverly's head suddenly appears from the middle doorway. "Well, hello, son." He walks along the wall, lifts a hinged piece of countertop at the end, and comes out to shake my hand. "How can I help you?"

"My name is Sam Parsons."

"Eva's boy?"

"Yes, and I need to talk to you about the circumstances surrounding the death of Buster Munroe."

Frank looks suddenly serious. "Okay, then. Let's go on back to my office where we can talk." He lifts the hinged piece of countertop again, and I follow him into his office.

Sheriff Frank pulls the door closed behind us and says, "Have a seat." Then he plants himself behind his desk in a brown leather chair. Elbows on the armrests, fingers entwined, he leans back in the chair and says, "Okay, Sam Parsons, I'm all ears."

# Twenty-Six

My hands tremble as I set my laptop on Frank's desk, pictures on display. I peel back the cover of my notebook and clear my throat. I begin with the phone call. The aunts were clearly trying to keep Mom from coming up for the funeral. And when we arrived, we were greeted by the very detailed – way too detailed – story the aunts told about Uncle Buster's death.

Then I tell him about Barney Baldwin from the funeral home, and the bruises and injuries hidden by make-up, and the intentional positioning of the deceased in his pecan-wood casket. I explain that Barney claimed to have seen a will that designated Aunt Bess as executrix, even though *she* acted like she found the will *later*. More importantly, I point out, the signature was formed with large, round letters that in no way resemble Uncle Buster's handwriting.

I momentarily wish I had remembered to bring *The Haunted Mesa* with me, but I explain the whole signature difference to Sheriff Frank, and he nods slowly, his brown eyes fixed on me. "I can bring it to you and show you. I have it back at the inn," I tell him.

"That's all right. I believe you. Keep going."

So I continue. I take him on a brief journey through Bess Munroe's financial woes and establish a clear motive. Then I pull out all the stops. "Now, I know Jud Waverly is your brother, and I hate to make this personal, but he figures into this thing somehow." I proceed to tell him about Jud and Bess hugging in the garage, and about the dubious story of Jud seeing Uncle Buster from the road on his way to the Sunday evening church service.

Frank sighs, closes his eyes, and rubs his forehead like I've hit a nerve. I wait until he's looking. I don't want him to miss the big finish. When he leans back in his chair, eyes on me once again, I proceed.

I present the symptoms of arsenic poisoning and correlate them with the apparent sequence of Uncle Buster's demise. "I called the state medical examiner's office," I tell him. "I spoke with a man named Brian. He wouldn't divulge the results of the toxicology test, but I think we both know what that report says."

"We do?" Frank raises his eyebrows and looks genuinely befuddled.

"Yes," I say. I'm in this deep. Might as well finish it. I direct his attention to my laptop. "In this picture, you see Bess Munroe's large black handbag. If you look closely, you'll notice writing on the edge of a paper protruding from this manila folder." *And now, in for a landing.* "No doubt, she has obtained a copy of the toxicology report: *–senic ppb.* There's only one logical conclusion."

Sheriff Frank leans back and his leather swivel chair squeaks. He strokes the stubble on his chin and studies me carefully. Finally, he speaks. "Sam, you've done an impressive bit of investigative work here. If you stick around, I just might want to hire you."

"Thank you, sir." I'm wondering why we aren't grabbing the handcuffs and racing out to apprehend the suspect. But Frank just sits there. And then he says, "However, there are a few minor details you may have misinterpreted."

Now I'm the befuddled one. "Like what?"

"Well, let's start with that report. A toxicology report generally takes about six weeks to complete, and as far as I know, arsenic wouldn't show up in a blood sample. You'd need tissue for that. The report you saw was something different."

"But it definitely said *arsenic*." I'm standing my ground. No backing down.

"Hold on, now. Let me backtrack. When Mountain-Aire Homes found out they could acquire Buster's acreage, their plan was to clear the land and build a bunch of cabins they could rent. But before they could build, they had to get some inspections."

I nod like I'm following him, but he seems to be leading us off on a tangent.

"The crew they sent over from Raleigh tested the well water your Uncle Buster had been drinking. They found dangerous levels of arsenic in it."

"In the *well water*?" It never occurred to me that the aunts could have poisoned the well water, but I'm open for plot twists.

"Your Uncle Buster was a frugal man. He didn't want to pay for garbage pick-up."

"I know that," I tell him. "But I don't see how it's relevant."

Frank holds up a hand. "Well, let me finish. For many years, Buster loaded trash in the bed of his truck and hauled it to the dump. But, when that old pick-up of his was on its last leg, Buster decided to trade it in for a small car that got better gas mileage."

I'm trying to remain patient with Frank, but he's straying further and further from the murder.

"The problem was, he no longer had the bed of his truck to use for hauling garbage. So he came up with another plan. There's an old abandoned well about 30 feet from the one he used for water. Buster decided he would dump his trash in that abandoned well."

He pauses, and I don't know if he's expecting me to say something, so I do. "Maybe he was composting? At our house in Florida we have a compost bin..." I let my voice trail off because Frank is shaking his head.

"He wasn't composting. Mr. Munroe was dumping everything in that old well – food and household waste, as well as all kinds of containers – from his Meals on Wheels containers and old paint cans to empty bottles of weed killer and pesticide."

Suddenly, I feel like I've been punched in the gut and emptied of every thought, every word, every feeling. Frank gives it a minute to sink in. "But wait –" I finally ask, "if that

179

was all dumped in the *abandoned* well, how did it get into his drinking water?"

Frank takes another deep breath. "It looks like when Mr. Munroe had a new well drilled, he didn't go about the proper permitting. The new well was drilled too close to the old one, and there ended up being some hydraulic connectivity between the two."

Still numb, I'm trying to process what he's saying. Frank spells it out for me. "The poison was leaching into the groundwater and contaminating the water in the well he used for drinking. It had probably been making him sick for a while now."

My mind flashes to the water bottles covering the kitchen table, and the new coffee maker with its designated gallon jug of store-bought water. And next to it...the purse, the report... "So the report I saw sticking out of Aunt Bess's purse, the arsenic ppb, it was about the well water. It was from the inspection."

"Yep. I'm willing to bet that's what you saw. And if you put that information together with all your investigative work, I think we can see that if arsenic killed your Uncle Buster–"

"It was his own doing." I can't let him finish that sentence. It's painful to say, but it would be even more painful to hear. I stand up on wobbly legs and reach to shake the hand of Sheriff Frank Waverly. "Thank you for your time, sir."

He gives me a firm handshake and says, "You're mighty welcome. It's an honor to meet such a fine detective. You come see me if you're ever looking for some work in law enforcement."

Frank opens the door and ushers me out of his office. "Let me know if I can do anything else for you, Sam."

I walk toward the counter, but after a couple of steps, I pause. "Actually, there is something. Your brother, Jud, I saw him heading out of town today, and I couldn't help but notice a duffle bag that was stuffed pretty full. Is he away on a trip? I was hoping I'd get to tell him goodbye before we left." I don't actually want to tell him goodbye. I'm just curious.

"Well, now, that's real nice of you, Sam. I'll pass that along if he calls." Frank looks through the front window, and a fading afternoon shadow falls over his face. "It might be a while. Jud got his heart broken, *again*, by an old flame. At his age, he should be headin' into retirement, but instead, he and his guitar are headin' off to Nashville to chase a dream."

"Country music?"

"Gospel," Frank says.

I picture Jud's fervent rendition of "How Great Thou Art" and have to smile. "I hope that works out for him," I say. And I think I actually mean it.

The glass door with the gold Sheriff's star closes behind me, and I begin my trek back to the Mountaineer Inn. Frank's words roll through my mind, and I cringe at the thought of the old flame who broke Jud's heart...*again*. Aunt Bess, no doubt.

I walk past the diner and soak in the glow of fluorescent light. Inside, Fanny is counting up the money in the register, probably preparing to head home and let the dinner shift take over. I feel comfort in the warm familiarity of the place.

The feelings are different when I pass Weston Realty. The MOUNTAIN-AIRE HOMES sign looms large above the building and casts a long shadow across the emptiness where the pink Cadillac was parked just an hour ago. I shudder at the thought of my accusation that was cut off just in time.

I cross the vacant street and head back up toward the inn when my back pocket starts buzzing repeatedly. Annoyed that someone would call rather than text, I grab the phone, only to see Dad's contact picture staring back at me.

"Hello?"

"Where are you, son? We're back at the inn and your mother's worried sick!"

# Twenty-Seven

Dad meets me halfway up the hill, and for the rest of the walk back to the inn, he's ranting in the voice he generally reserves for football practice. Every mini-tirade is punctuated with the question, "What were you thinking?!"

Maybe I'm still a little numb from Sheriff Frank's news, but I'm surprisingly calm. I feel justified. Indignant, even. I was looking for answers, and I found them.

As we approach the room, Mom is standing in the doorway, teary-eyed but smiling. She hugs me. Classic good cop, bad cop. "Let's go inside and talk." She seems weary. And I'm probably about to make it worse.

We sit facing each other on the two double beds of our deluxe room. They listen, Dad maintaining the warden persona and Mom still somewhat frail, as I begin to tell them what I've learned.

I show them the pictures. Dad rubs his face, exasperated, but Mom leans in. She sees it, too: *-eport* and *–senic ppb*. "At first, I thought it confirmed my suspicion that Aunt Bess – and maybe even Aunt Bertie– had poisoned Uncle Buster. So I called the Office of the Medical Examiner, sure that this report was the analysis of that vial of blood."

They raise their eyebrows simultaneously, but neither one speaks, so I continue. I tell them about my conversation with Brian from Toxicology, and explain that my next logical step was to talk to law enforcement. "So I went to see Sheriff Waverly."

Dad blows up. "You walked all the way to the Sheriff's Office?"

Mom reaches out and touches my hand. "You talked to Frank?"

I go on to tell them about my conversation with Sheriff Frank, and I can't help but notice they don't seem surprised by any of my revelations. No furrowed brows, no audible gasps. I tread gingerly into the part about the old abandoned well. Tears fall silently from Mom's eyes, and Dad drops his gaze to the floor, but again, no signs of shock. I finish my briefing and we sit in silence for a long minute or two.

Finally, I feel the need to speak. "The will, though. I know it can't be his signature, and there's still no way the property should belong—"

Dad sighs and holds a hand up to stop me. "We discussed that with the lawyer who looked over the real estate offer. He discouraged us from pursuing a challenge to the will."

"But Dad, it's not fair—"

"Now, hang on," he interrupts. "Let me finish."

I take a deep breath and stifle my comments. Dad continues.

"He said families often squabble over wills, but it's hard to prove fraud. He said it's not worth pursuing unless there's an alternate will."

I can't help myself. My thoughts erupt into words. "They cleaned up Uncle Buster's house and got rid of lots of his papers! If a different will existed, they probably destroyed it!"

Mom reaches out, puts a steadying hand on my knee, and Dad speaks slowly, deliberately. "The will looks legitimate, and it's witnessed by Sheriff Waverly's wife."

"But—"

It's Mom who cuts me off this time. "Geraldine Waverly grew up with Bess. She trusted her. Perhaps she didn't actually *see* Uncle Buster sign the will, but I'm sure she erred on the side of compassion. Everyone knew Uncle Buster didn't trust lawyers."

I can't believe Mom can be so calm and understanding. *Where is the outrage?* "So what happens now?" I'm losing hope of any justice.

Dad says, "Well, your mother learned quite a lot from ringing Rita." He can't help but grin a little when he says that. "It seems Mountain-Aire Homes is not only pulling the plug on developing Uncle Buster's property; they're pulling out of Ashe County altogether."

It's the first good news I've heard all day.

Mom sits up and smiles. "It seems the combination of hostile neighbors and contaminated water was just too much. They're looking for another site for the development."

"So June gets her home back?" I have to ask. I'm grasping for a silver lining here.

Mom's smile fades and Dad picks up the conversation. "Not exactly. It seems another buyer scooped it up already."

"How do you know all this?"

"Rita," they say in unison.

Mom continues. "Rita talked to Bud Weston, owner of Weston Realty. He told her all about the arsenic in the well, and with that and the acres of dirt Jud cleared, the land is not worth much right now. He planned to meet with Aunt Bess this afternoon to discuss a drastic price reduction."

"But the aunts still get to cash in and disappear. It doesn't seem fair."

"Well..." Mom begins. She pauses and looks to Dad. He nods and she continues. "You were right about Aunt Bess having financial troubles. It seems she was trying to worm her way back in with her old beau, Jud Waverly, probably hoping that he could bankroll her recovery. If Uncle Buster had found out about her sneaking down here to visit Jud on the weekends, he'd have blown a gasket." Mom rolls her eyes and shakes her head. "When she found out Jud didn't actually have any money, she dropped him – *again*!"

"Wait – so when he lied about seeing Uncle Buster through the window—"

"Probably a cover," Dad says. "Just in case somebody had spotted Bess or that unmistakable pink sedan. She wouldn't want them to know she came to town and didn't even check on her brother when..." His voice trails off and he looks at the floor.

I'm practically speechless.

This time Dad looks at Mom and she gives the nod. "Seems like Bess is in some serious debt. We think she was hoping Jud could help her out of it. But things didn't work out that way. She's headed home to face her troubles, and she needs money to help with that."

"You got all this from Rita?"

Dad smiles. "She has a way of getting people to talk."

There's so much to process. My head is pounding, and my shoulders are tense. I lean back on the bed to stretch out and think.

I'm scared to ask the questions echoing in the hollow space of my head. *Are we seriously considering buying Uncle Buster's place? Are we the kind of people who can afford a vacation home? Or do we plan to move here? Are we committing to cleaning up and restoring the property?* I don't even know if I want the answers right now.

As if reading my mind, Dad interrupts my anxiety-ridden thought-spiral and says, "Hang on, there. We haven't gotten to the best part." I reluctantly pull my body up from the mattress and I'm met with wacky smiles. My parents are delirious.

"Back to June," Mom says. "Once Bud Weston talks Bess down on the price, we want to turn the offer over to June."

I'm intrigued.

"I know it's not perfect. She won't get her home back, but she can start fresh and make Uncle Buster's place her very own. The money she has from the sale of her dad's property should leave her with a sizeable nest egg."

187

Suddenly, it's like a curtain is lifting and sunlight is streaming into the darkness. Something really good could come from all this.

"The only problem," Dad says, "is it'll be a lot of work to restore the land. She needs help."

"Hang on," I say with a smile. "Warblers!"

Mom and Dad voice their confusion in unison. "Warblers?"

I open my laptop and pull up the research from my bird report. And there it is. Contact information for the Golden-winged Warbler Working Group. "I know just who to call," I tell them.

# Twenty-Eight

It's been six weeks since the deal went down. June bought Buster's place for a steal, and she's been painting, redecorating, and of course, replanting blueberry bushes in front of the house. And she's going strictly organic.

The early successional forest habitat is being restored on the property, thanks in part to the Golden-winged Warbler Working Group. They got Audubon North Carolina involved, and their High Country chapter sent a conservation biologist out to see the property. Audubon volunteers, led by the owner of the Four Square Diner, helped June replant the leveled acres with native grasses and shrubs to create an optimum golden-winged warbler habitat.

June got so excited about the birds that she got her neighbors in on the conservation efforts. She organized a meeting at her house for anyone who wanted information about maintaining a bird-friendly yard.

Of course, Carl was there. And another neighbor came, too. It turns out the new owner of June's old home is none other than skinny-tie-guy Kyle Jasper.

Kyle no longer works with the Mountain-Aire group. He's now employed by Weston Realty, and he's an entrepreneur on the side. His latest business venture is called "Mountain Muffins," and he's been able to place his product in stores and diners across four counties. He finally talked Fanny into it.

Apparently, Kyle is quite the persuasive fellow. He also talked June and Carl into setting up Wi-Fi connections, and they've been on an email frenzy, giving us the play-by-play on every detail of the Ashe County saga.

And so, here we are, finally taking that trip to the Pro Football Hall of Fame. Of course, on the drive from Jacksonville, Florida, to Canton, Ohio, we know the perfect place to stop over for a night.

We get a deluxe room at the Mountaineer Inn. Dad immediately sits at the table and checks his email while Mom freshens up.

"Hey, check this out," Dad says. "Apparently, Rita's Realty has club seats at all the Jaguars games. Coach Kelly said they'll be out of town for the first exhibition game, and he's wondering if we'd like their tickets."

I bolt to the table and join him. "You're saying yes, right?"

"You betcha!" He sends an immediate reply and smiles at me. "There are four tickets. Why don't you see if Oscar would like to join us?"

After my brief, emoji-filled text exchange with Oscar, we walk to the pizza place next to the Sheriff's Office. It was my special request. The pizza is thin and cheesy, with little pools of grease settled in each slice of pepperoni. Just the way I like it.

As I take a bite and work to sever a stretchy string of cheese, I notice a familiar face across the way. It's none other than Byron Hicks, of the Law Office of Hicks and Honeycutt. He's dining alone, unless you count the briefcase, laptop, and notebook.

Byron eats his pizza with a knife and a fork, cutting each slice into tiny segments and keeping the grease far from his fingers. He's in his crisply pressed jeans, dress shirt, and sockless Italian loafers again. Must be his Saturday uniform. I almost feel sorry for the guy. If he ever looked up from his work, I might just send him a friendly wave.

After what was, in my opinion, a quite satisfying meal, we step out into the warm evening and begin our leisurely stroll back to the Mountaineer Inn.

"I'm glad we decided to walk," Mom says. "The exercise might offset the grease we just consumed." Dad smiles and nudges me, but she just keeps talking. "We should pick up something to take to brunch tomorrow."

Dad looks at his watch. "It's getting late. Besides, June invited us to brunch. Doesn't that mean she's doing the cooking?"

"Oh, Bob, really!" Mom stomps her foot on the sidewalk and we all stop. Coincidentally, we are right in front of the Four Square Diner, and in the window, there's a sign that reads: WE SELL MOUNTAIN MUFFINS. $1 EACH OR $10 FOR A DOZEN.

The tension is immediately suspended and we're soon carrying a dozen of Fanny's blueberry muffins back to our deluxe room. Well, we're also carrying three individual muffins in a bag because Mom feels the need to be *proactive*. In other words, she doesn't trust us.

Sunday mornings in the mountains are quiet. Some church bells ring and a few fitness warriors are out for runs or bike rides, but for the most part, human noise is at a minimum. The air is filled with birdsong and breezes. I can hear the things I normally take for granted. The gentle rustle of leaves. The frantic movement of squirrels. The rhythmic tapping of a woodpecker in the distance. Even my own breath and heartbeat seem amplified by the absence of human movement.

We don't need to be at June's house until 10:00, so we take it slow. Sleep late, enjoy a blueberry muffin, and ride around town with the Jeep windows rolled down. And this time I'm paying attention. Like I never have before. The morning sun smears shades of pink across the sky. It sends a warm glow down over the mountains, making them look more green than gray in this early light.

We venture to the outskirts of town, past the Ashe County Funeral Home, Ralph's Limousine Rentals, and the Piggly Wiggly. We pass a giant metal rooster, a mural painted on a brick wall, a church made of stone, and a bunch of signs I've never noticed before. There's a sign that points in the direction of the Solid Waste Management Facility. Rows and rows of Christmas trees line a hillside behind a sign that reads TRINA'S

TREE FARM. Cows and goats graze in a pasture behind a sign that points to a local cheese factory. Why have I never noticed these things before?

Finally, Dad winds back around to the road that leads up the mountain. And we climb. Past farms and houses, chicken coops and trailers, until we round a steep curve and see a red brick chimney rising out of the hillside. The mailbox still says "Route 6, Box 322," but it's not the hand-painted script I'm used to. The letters and numbers are printed on big stickers and surrounded by hand-painted flowers.

We make a sharp left onto the rocky driveway. Rows of blueberry bushes once again line the hillside in front of the one-story brick house. We swing a sharp right where there used to be a crabapple tree, and we're met with a surprise. Several cars line the flat area near the garage.

Dad parks the Jeep next to a white pick-up with a Weston Realty bumper sticker and says, "I didn't know there'd be other guests."

Mom stares at the house and mumbles, "Maybe we should have picked up more muffins." But I don't think a potential muffin shortage is what's captivated her mind. I think it's the house.

Uncle Buster's once-dusty front porch with its two folding lawn chairs has been transformed. There are two white rocking chairs on either side of a square wooden table. Hanging baskets overflow with blooms, and a "Welcome" sign hangs on the door above a colorful mat.

We step out of the Jeep and marvel at the acres of green. How did it happen so fast? Tall grasses sway, goldenrod blooms, and young shrubs are placed here and there, growing dark and thick. In front of it all stands a sign that says "Shrubland," with the silhouette of a little songbird perched on the letter $n$.

The mesmerizing moment is broken by a voice calling from the front porch. "You made it! Come on in!" June is standing on the mat, hand on the doorknob. She wears a dress covered with sunflowers, her long hair is twisted up into a fancy knot, and her once shadowy eyes sparkle.

We move in unison, drawn by June's light. We hug and greet and talk about how great the place looks. Soon we're surrounded by the brunch crowd, all gathered to see us. They laugh and chat and reach out like one unit – a community moving in sync.

Kyle takes the box from Dad's hands and places it on the kitchen table. "Mountain Muffins – you're a man with impeccable taste!" Fanny is at his side. She blushes, laughs, and slaps him playfully on the shoulder.

The church ladies are there, busying themselves in the kitchen. "Try the sausage and hash brown casserole," one of them says to me. She shoves a paper plate in my hands and pushes me toward the food.

"You're a growing boy! You need to eat!" the second one says.

The third one pats my hand and solemnly offers, "We all went to the early service so we could be here to see your mama."

As I make my way around the table, the trio corners Mom, peppering her with comments and questions.

"Money trouble. That's what we heard."

"Poor Jud. Heartbroken again."

"Do you know if Bertie's son ever found a job?"

Mom doesn't have a chance to respond because their words are being fired at her in rapid succession. Finally, Carl breaks up the mob. "Ladies, let the woman get her food and leave the gossip out of this."

"Oh, it's not gossip," the first church lady declares.

The second one follows with, "We need all the details so we know exactly what to pray for."

"Be sure to try the sausage and hash brown casserole," the third one says. They're really pushing that casserole.

Carl smiles, puts an arm around Mom's shoulder, and ushers her to the table.

Soon we're all seated in the living room, where flowery throw pillows are scattered about on blue and yellow cushions. There's a rapping on the door. June looks out the window from the white glider rocker that has claimed the space once occupied by Uncle Buster's favorite yellow chair. She shouts, "Frank and Geraldine, you know you don't have to knock. Come on in!"

Sheriff Frank and his wife enter in their church clothes, arms loaded with fresh flowers and fruit. They deposit their bounty on the table and proceed with gracious hugs and handshakes, finding a way to personalize each greeting. Frank asks Kyle about the real estate market, and Geraldine asks Fanny about her muffin business. Frank talks to June about the county water and waste management service while Geraldine offers lavish praise to the church ladies for the way they can organize a brunch.

Finally, Frank asks Dad about his prospects for the new football season, and Geraldine talks to Mom about her book club's latest selection. Literature is a subject that sucks Mom in, so while they continue to talk, Sheriff Frank shakes my hand. "Sam the man. Solve any crimes lately?"

I feel the heat of embarrassment rise in my face, but Frank goes on to tell Dad, "The boy has the makings of a great detective. Or maybe a great reporter."

Dad says, "He's had his sights set on ESPN for years now; we'll see what happens." And then, thankfully, they're back to football.

As the chatter in the room continues, I slip out onto the front porch for some air. I sit in a white rocker and look across the blueberry bushes to the mailbox. I think about the many times we've turned that corner and headed up the rocky driveway. I whisper into the empty air, "Uncle Buster, I guess I cracked the case. But it didn't end quite like one of your Louis L'Amour novels. I wish–"

But I can't finish the sentence. What do I wish? *I wish you were here? I wish you would've paid for garbage pick-up? I wish I had gotten to know you better?*

Suddenly, the muffled voices behind me erupt into a fit of laughter and I wonder who told the joke. I stand, ready to leave my thoughts and rejoin the party when out of nowhere, a huge breeze kicks up and rustles the acres of tall grass. It moves across the porch and dances through the blueberry bushes before traveling down the driveway.

I stand frozen, eyes on the road, as if I'm watching every apprehension, every question within me being swept away. Stillness returns. Sunlight and warmth bathe the scene. And then, like magic, a golden-winged warbler perches on the mailbox and sings.

## The Golden Winged Warbler

This book is a work of fiction, but a few things in it are true. For example, Jacksonville, Florida, really has a football team called the Jacksonville Jaguars. You probably knew that. Ashe County, North Carolina, is a real place (even though the town where you find the Mountaineer Inn and the Four-Square Diner is completely a product of my imagination). And perhaps most wonderful of all, Golden-winged Warblers are real.

The Golden-winged Warbler is a migratory songbird, preferring to spend winter months in places like South America. By late April, they return to various regions of the Appalachian  Mountains and eastern Canada. Like most birds, the females' markings are not as splashy as the males'. Males have white bellies, gray backs, patches of yellow on their wings, little yellow caps above their eyes, and tufts of black on their throats. (That's what led Sam to call them "blackbeards.") They eat mostly insects, and they make a lot of high-pitched sounds that seem to buzz or vibrate. Actually, they kind of sound like insects.

If you choose to visit the National Audubon Society's website (https://www.audubon.org/birds/priority), which I highly encourage you to do, you will find that there is indeed a list of Priority Birds. At the top of that page, you will see these words: "Audubon's priority bird species are birds of significant conservation need, for which our actions, over time, can lead to measurable improvements in status."

These words are very true. Many beautiful birds are losing their habitats, and without their habitats, these bird populations will continue to dwindle. But their story doesn't have to have a sad ending.

Many people care deeply about protecting these priority birds, and there are things we can do to help. The best first step is to learn about the birds. For instance, you can immerse yourself in interesting facts about the Golden-winged Warbler, whose scientific name is *Vermivora chrysoptera*. Once a thriving species in the eastern United States, the number of these beautiful songbirds has steadily decreased over many years. There are several reasons for a decline in their population, but one of those reasons is certainly loss of habitat.

Golden-winged Warblers, as Sam discovered, live in an early successional habitat. They like brushy areas with scattered tree growth. These areas are often found on the edges of forests or where land that had been cleared is growing back to its natural state. The Golden-winged Warbler Working Group (which is entirely real -- I didn't make it up) developed a conservation plan that includes the restoration and expansion of habitats for these priority songbirds. They provide training workshops, teach people about habitat management, and continually monitor the success of their efforts. They coordinate their strategies with regional Young Forest Initiatives, another conservation group doing really good work to restore early successional habitats.

If you would like to learn more about Golden-winged Warblers or the efforts to help them survive and thrive, you can visit the list of websites provided here. Of course, you will probably end up discovering other wonderful birds as well, and you might even put one of them in a book, should you decide to write one. (Please let me know if you do. I would definitely like to read it.) Happy birding!

National Audubon Society Priority Birds:
https://www.audubon.org/birds/priority

Golden-winged Warbler Working Group: http://gwwa.org/

The Young Forest Project: https://youngforest.org/

## Acknowledgments

This book is the product of writing and revising, parsing and pruning, resting and returning, over and over again. But it was not a solitary process. I must thank my students at Holy Comforter Episcopal School for listening, providing feedback, and being the world's greatest critique group. Additionally, I am grateful to others who invested themselves in the process: literary luminaries Sandra Wylie and Rosanne Reanier, author Chris Low, beta reader Judy Fiedler, and editor-extraordinaire M.R. Street.

I am more broadly grateful for the support of good friends and an amazing family. We may be spread out, but physical distance means little when you are close in heart. And my heart is full to overflowing. I dedicated this book to my sisters, Joan Walton, Judy Fiedler, and Shirley Sapp. The memories and experiences that weave themselves into the creative process are not mine alone; they are memories and experiences that belong to my sisters as well.

I am inspired daily by the talent and drive of my children, who happen to all be adults now: Tyler, joyful adventurer; Dylan, entrepreneur and mother to the world's most precious children (I might be biased); Emily, soon-to-be PhD and world-changer; Shelby, the phenomenal artist responsible for this book's beautiful cover; and Hillary, a busy college freshman with mad camera skills (and the grace to take many headshots so we could find just the right one).

I am thankful daily for my partner in life, my husband John. He brings me coffee every morning, cooks dinner every night, keeps the technology running, and knows when to whisk me away from the computer and onto a lovely adventure. I am blessed beyond measure.

Finally, I am grateful to readers everywhere. Through reading, we share, we grow, and we connect. Thank you for sharing, growing, and connecting with me.

## About the Author

Susan Koehler is the author of four professional development resources for teachers and six books for children. *Dahlia in*

*Bloom,* her first novel for young readers, received
a starred review from Kirkus Reviews and a gold
medal in the Florida Authors and Publishers
Association President's Book Awards. When not
writing, Susan can be found enjoying outdoor
activities with her adventurous husband or
spending as much time as possible with her five
very busy children and two adorable grandchildren. Contact
Susan at susankoehlerwrites.com or turtlecovepress.com.

Made in the USA
Columbia, SC
14 July 2021